The Wuhan Plague

("Sleepless in Wuhan")

By James Crew Allen and Richard Bonte

THE WUHAN PLAGUE, ("Sleepless in Wuhan") by
James Crew Allen and Richard Bonte

PROLOGUE

May 2020

I looked down at the big white ambulances, their sirens screaming, flashing down the center of 34th St., and out through the tunnel under the East River and over to Queens. I was so high up in my building, the New York City cabs below looked like yellow miniature toys scampering to get out of the way of the charging dead. I switched on the TV to block out the racket but now the blare of the sirens was coming through the speakers as well because that's all there was on TV: Corona/Covid-19, Covid-19/Corona.

Fully masked people in blue uniforms with purple surgical gloves and face guards were running about pell-mell in a military type field hospital. Outside the emergency entrance, ambulances were pulling up three at a time. Orderlies and nurses, some of them not even wearing proper protective clothing were loading coughing and choking patients onto stretchers and looking for vacant hospital beds. These were filling up fast.

A man with his face mask fogging up, his chest heaving and his head twisted unnaturally to the side, was fighting for air.

"He's dying. Quick! Get the ventilator."

Another ventilator was wheeled up; there weren't many left, and the stretchers were lined up outside.

"Soon there won't be enough. [BLEEP], it's no use."

There was another wave of blue uniforms, masks, gloves and covered shoes, all running and walking in different directions.

The man's body was now convulsing; his face was thrashing from side to side. It was all the orderly could do to attach the ventilator. The orderly was worried about his own mask being yanked off as the dying man grasped for something, anything to survive. Finally, the ventilator tube was in place, and the orderly backed off to watch.

But it was no use. The man's heart was failing him. Despite his new oxygen tube, he was literally being asphyxiated.

The monitor flatlined, and the orderly now began giving the dying patient a massive amount of cardiac massage. It seemed to last forever, but it was only ninety seconds.

And that was it.

I switched off the TV. I could not take it anymore. I sat quietly for a moment and began to remind myself of the wonderful days in what now seemed like a bygone era. Stanford and our graduation, summer at the beach.

Whatever happened to David Cheng ? He was working in Wuhan, wasn't he?

CHAPTER ONE – "LITTLE CHINA GIRL"

Stanford University, Early June 2018

David Cheng grabbed a tray and plate and stood in front of his microbiology advisor who was grilling hamburgers on the barbeque. David wasn't used to seeing his advisor in this light, with his large white "cook's" hat and bright red gloves. Normally he was dressed in an upscale, casual way and stood in front of the white board drawing organic formulas for his students.

"I'll have a burger with swiss cheese, if you don't mind, Dr. Reinhardt, and maybe some of those onion rings, too. Thanks," said David as he extended his plate.

Professor Reinhardt loaded David's plate with a burger, onions, potato salad and a perfectly grilled sesame seed bun.

"I'll be sad to see you go, David. You've been more helpful to me than a fourth-year doctoral student. Are you going to work or study, or do both next year?"

"I'm first going to take a short vacation on the Gulf Coast in Florida. Then it's back to Hong Kong and see my parents. I've been offered a great research job at the World Health Organization, but I'd like to first talk things over with my dad. The fees at Stanford have really set me back, and I need to make some money, pronto."

"The WHO? Wow, that's a great place to work. Geneva, Switzerland!"

"I'm not sure yet. But whatever it is, I'll definitely need your recommendation, Dr. Reinhardt."

"Anything I can do to help. Research is your strong suit, David. Epidemiology is important what with the relatively recent SARS and Ebola outbreaks. The WHO does the best research in the world in epidemiology. I think you should take that position."

"Thanks for the tip," said David taking a bite of his burger. "Have you ever been a chef, Dr. Reinhardt? This tastes great."

"I'm a chemist by trade, David. Cooking and all the rest is just a sideline of chemistry. Go have a seat with your friends."

Little groups of four or five graduating seniors sat around picnic tables spread out amongst the eucalyptus trees. A huge cardinal and white banner featuring the words "Class of 2018" stretched out between two of the groups. Stanford was no longer the farm it had been back in the day that Leland Stanford and his wife had it built in 1885 for their only son Leland Jr. who had died the year before of typhus. As per the founders' vision, it was still a nonsectarian and co-educational institution although no longer a very affordable one. Just to enter Stanford was a Herculean task with its four percent acceptance rate. One had to be extremely intelligent and preferably a member of one of the many diverse groups on campus.

David Cheng was one such person. An extremely bright individual with an IQ of 160 and a weighted grade point average of 5.2 out of 4.0, he also played the cello and was an excellent volleyball player. He had belonged to a top service organization—the Kiwanis Club— in his high school in Hong Kong where he had grown up, the son of a Chinese father and white American mother. He was tall and good-looking and had an easygoing personality which hid the fact that he was very hardworking and industrious. He was the perfect four percent candidate.

One thing David did not like was too much sun so he cast his eye around for a shady spot and saw a group of people seated under a palm tree.

"David, get over here, will you?"

It was Jesse Owens, the key spiker on their volleyball team and someone he occasionally went to the beach with at Santa Cruz to play two-on-two beach volleyball. Owens was an aeronautical engineer.

"How's the future savior of our human race doing?"

"We could say that about you, too, Mr. Rocket Scientist!" said David, straddling the picnic bench and taking a bite of his hamburger, "and even when you're busy spiking the ball."

"Hey, David."

"How's it going, guy?"

"You good?"

There was a chorus of greetings from the different members of his close friends whom he probably wouldn't see too much of after he went to Hong Kong and then on to Europe.

David greeted them all but there was one person he didn't know and she was seated almost opposite him.

"Do you know Xi Di Wan, David?" asked Jesse.

"Can't say I do," said David. "Hi, my name's David Cheng. Nî hâo ma. Pleased to meet you."

"Nî hâo ma. And I preased to meet chyu," said Xi Di Wan in heavily accented English. Xi Di Wan had shoulder-length black hair parted on the side. She was slim and tall for a Chinese girl, 5'7". She was both pretty and serious; she studied David intently when he wasn't looking at her, but would peep down or away when he did.

A few seconds went by as they looked around. Then they studied each other at the same time and suddenly went into their native Mandarin. David's accent was quite different from hers. All Jesse noticed was that he had suddenly been excluded from the conversation, but David said quickly, "Excuse us, Jesse, let me talk to her in Chinese for a bit and then we'll get back to the party!" To her credit, Xi Di Wan told Jesse the same thing with a hand gesture and then reverted to studying David.

"Where are you from?" David asked her in Mandarin.

"I'm from Beijing," she answered.

"Funny," he said, "You sound like you're from Wuhan."

"Oh, maybe because my parents are from there," she replied. "Do you know a lot of people in China?"

"Not really, most of the people I know are from Hong Kong. But I've met some scientists from Wuhan that lecture frequently in Hong Kong and the United States. They are the leading experts in my field."

"Really!" she replied. "What is your field?"

"Epidemiology," David responded. "Do you know it?"

"Sure, I know it. My mother's a doctor."

"That's funny," David answered, "Both my parents are doctors! We have a lot in common."

"What are you doing after graduation?"

"I've got a job at the World Health Organization in Geneva, but if that doesn't work out, maybe I'll come back here and do research."

"As a grad student?" she said. "You're not sick of it here yet?"

"Of California! You're asking me? That's a funny question from a Chinese girl," David said, "What about you? Are you a student here?"

"I've been here on a six-month sabbatical in the business school."

"The business of America is business! Calvin Coolidge said that. No better place for studying business in the world. Oh, in case you didn't know, Calvin Coolidge was the thirtieth president of the United States in the 1920's."

"Of course I knew, David. He also said it takes a great man to be a great listener."

"It follows that it takes a great listener to be a great man."

"Or a great woman!"

"Definitely. I'm listening! To you, Di Wan. Some people say the place to do business today is China. But I don't think so unless your father is a member of the Chinese Communist Party. If not, you really struggle."

Xi Di Wan smiled bleakly, her eyes dull.

"Let me guess, your father is a member of the Communist Party?"

"Yes."

"So you could never live in Taiwan?"

"Taiwan is a renegade state, David."

David felt uncomfortable with this response, but banished it from his thoughts as he really liked Xi.

"When are you going back to China?"

"Tomorrow morning!"

"Oh, so soon? I'm sorry."

"The sorrow's mine since I've really enjoyed talking to you." She looked at her watch and said, "That reminds me, I have to pack."

The twinkle was back in her eye.

She bent over very close to David to shake his hand and said, "I wish you the very best in your chosen career and hopefully we will meet again."

With that she smiled, said good-bye to Jesse, waved vaguely to the others and sauntered off to the parking lot. Jesse looked at David,

"Funny, dude, I seem to hear samba music playing in the background while your Chinese 'Girl from Ipanema' just walks away."

CHAPTER TWO – LIFE'S A BEACH

July 2018 – Siesta Key Beach, Sarasota, Florida

David uncovered the simple sheet on his side of the bed, swung his feet over, sat up, stretched and yawned. His feet landed on a pink bra and matching panties that he picked up and placed on the night table. He looked over and patted her firm butt right where a ray of sunlight had pushed through a broken slat in the plantation shutters.

"Come on, Gina, time to rise and shine."

He leaned over and kissed her cheek. She was out cold.

He hoisted himself up, and made his way to the bathroom over a path of strewn clothes. He relieved himself, brushed his teeth, donned a pair of gym shorts and pushed through to the kitchen. Within minutes, David had prepared toast, fruit, cereal and orange juice and two cappuccinos with his Nespresso machine. Within those same minutes, Gina had stumbled through to the bathroom, washed and dressed and made her way to the kitchen.

They sat down and looked out onto a huge expanse of white sand that stretched a good hundred feet to the water. David's beach rental was small and run down but one side of the extra-large kitchen was all picture window that faced due west. In the morning, the rising sun from the east bleached out everything; in the evening, the sand was brown, red and gold as the locals watched the daily sunset from behind their cocktails.

David had discovered that there were only two times to play volleyball in the atrocious Florida heat: in the morning at six am or twelve hours later at six pm.

It was presently 5:45 am and already seventy-five degrees. By noon, it would be up to at least ninety-five. Even by eight am when they would have finished, the temperature was expected to rise to eighty-five with seventy percent humidity. Then it would be time to take a shower, close up the blinds and let the air conditioning take over. Gina would go to work at Starbucks, and David would prepare his online *Principles of Advanced Virology* class that he had taken on for a Pre-Geneva summer project for the World Health Organization.

David noted that the volleyballers had already arrived. He figured that he only needed thirty minutes to get ready, including breakfast, and he would be playing ball with some of the best beach volleyballers in the world.

He nodded to Gina and they made their barefoot way onto the sand. She was tall and slim and young with sandy blond hair and deep blue eyes—she couldn't have been more than eighteen—with only the smallest of tattoos on her right butt cheek. She had stood out since she wasn't sporting the huge disfiguring tattoos that everyone else had. As Cristiano Ronaldo, the good-looking megastar soccer player from Portugal had modestly once said, "If you have a Ferrari, do you plaster it with bumper stickers?"

David had met Gina the day before on the volleyball court, and she seemed to know everyone. At Siesta Key, there was Jim and Dave, Mike and Tony, Gina and Debbie or the Latins like Raul and Alonsa and Claudia, or even the black players like Gainell or Bunsen T. Nobody bothered with last names. Here today, gone tomorrow, Siesta Key was a continual summer party.

Gina would be attending FSU, Florida State University, in the fall up in Tallahassee. She was sweet but a bit young for him, and he felt nothing but physical attraction to her, which was not something to sneeze at. He had been sowing his wild oats all summer, and she was just starting her mating journey.

Gina was a young local who worked summer jobs, quite unlike the crazy Canadian, German and UK tourists who would lie on the beach and burn lobster red. David would notice them on his way to work lolling about on their beer guts in the hot white sand. David had a summer job as a boatman. He would prepare and repair small boats for tourists who wanted to fish or sightsee along the Sarasota Bay. Often they would ask him where to go to eat Mahi-Mahi or where the Ringling Circus Museum was. This was before they got sunburned. After, David would not see them again as they remained inside rental cars and literally saved their skins.

David's job didn't pay him much but it was enough for him to afford his rental, save some money for Geneva and especially pay for his air tickets to Geneva and Hong Kong. David needed to wind down after many years in school. David's working holiday in Siesta Key was turning out to be one of the best *working* vacations he had ever had.

"Can you take me to work now, Dave?" said Gina as she donned her Starbuck's uniform. It was only 8:30 am now, but they had played two hours of tough volleyball, taken a hot shower, made love again and were now getting dressed for the day. They piled into David's old Ford pick-up and drove through the steamy heat to the local Starbucks on the beach.

He dropped her off. With luck, his truck would make it back to his beach house without breaking down. He thought about all the freedoms Americans enjoyed without even giving it a second thought. It was not like that in Hong Kong.

By the time six pm had arrived, David was ready for more volleyball. Despite his long day, he was looking forward to seeing Gina and the acquaintances he was starting to call his *friends*. But Gina was not there. Instead, an almost older carbon copy of Gina with thick blond hair under a bright red baseball cap and matching bathing suit was spiking the ball in her place. What was interesting about this new girl was her spike. She had a terrific jump and tremendous power. And she played intelligently, too. Sometime she would set up to spike but then, at the last minute, tip it over the outstretched arms of the blocker on the other side. She had to have played Division One ball somewhere or even professional beach volleyball. And she was beautiful as well. He didn't like himself for thinking like this, but wasn't it convenient that Gina had not shown up?

They played an hour of volleyball and the gang of Jim and Mike and Tony et al. sat down for some *beerski's* on the front of Dave's rental unit. David took a sip of his Corona and looked around. Not only had Gina not phoned to tell him she was not coming, *Karen*, the top-notch volleyball player in the red-hot bikini, was sitting right next to him as if she had taken the young girl's place. Karen had a surprisingly melodious voice, and yet, like most Americans when you meet them was firing off question after question as if she were an employer interviewing a job applicant.

David was the applicant, and he enjoyed being so because he felt this girl really wanted to know all about him, and yet they had only been talking for fifteen minutes.

After a while David went inside to pee, but when he came back out, Karen was gone.

Another one gone? He looked around in the dimming light and didn't see her. The party was still raging and David looked lost. He pulled out a Corona longneck from the fridge and called Gina.

Karen had meanwhile crossed the road and swiftly approached a parked Jeep. She stopped at the rear entrance, and looked over her shoulder to ensure none of the volleyball players could see her. In the dark light it would have been impossible unless she had been followed.

She banged on the door which opened. She stepped inside, nodded to the two men who were in the back of the Jeep, and took off her baseball cap and blond wig.

"OK, let's go," said one of the men as he removed his headphones and hung them on the computer screen.

CHAPTER THREE – HONG KONG BOUND

Hong Kong, September 2018

David stepped out of the taxi and took in the panoramic view of Hong Kong's Victoria Harbour next to the Financial District. The view was breathtaking. Growing up, he had marveled at the many shades of blue, red, white and green streaks on the water at night, contrasting with the simple golden rays of sun glistening on the skyscrapers during the day.

He was standing at the base of a tall, shimmering steel and aluminum colossus extending thirty stories up where his father had bought their penthouse many years before. As beautiful as the view was from where he was standing, it was nothing compared to the one from their living room.

David waved his magnetic key over the sensor to the ground floor lobby. Huge modern art tableaux hung on the walls; a modern but low volume, bass heavy electro funk music pumped through the sound system signaling one could be anywhere and nowhere. He waved his key over another sensor and into a huge elevator car with a panoramic view.

David shot up in the car, the shaft of which was strategically placed on the outside of the building and encased in thick glass and aluminum extrusions. He experienced vertigo as he looked down instead of out over the harbor as his mouth opened wide to catch his excitement. Within seconds it seemed he was already on the thirtieth floor. Before he left the elevator, he gazed at the magnificent view of the harbor. On the left, he saw the Victoria Peak Tower, and in the distance, a building with "Getty" written on it.

He knocked on the ornate door of the only home he had ever known until the age of eighteen. Now, Mama and Papa were hugging and kissing him as they brought him over to the tea table filled with cakes, nuts and champagne. Mama pulled out a large "Graduation Card" and Papa popped some "Ruinart" champagne,

"Congratulations to our Graduate!" it read and they called out the same words, in unison,

"Congratulations to our Graduate!"

They all raised and clinked their glasses. David sat down in the firm comfortable armchair that he had always loved, and gazed again at the harbor. For the first time since his trip began thirty-six hours ago, he could relax and enjoy the view.

"How was your trip?" said Mama serving him a madeleine and scone, "You must be exhausted."

"You're right, Mama, normally I'd be sleeping and it would be yesterday."

"How *was* your graduation? I'm so proud of you!" said Papa, "you're a Stanford graduate now! Ready to go to medical school?"

"Actually, no, Papa, I want to be an epidemiologist and do viral research. In fact, and this may sound a little bit conceited on my part, I want to save humanity from pandemics like the SARS virus or Ebola."

"So you want to be a doctor?" said Papa, "you want to help people?"

"Yes, Papa, I do want to help people, but I want to do research and let science do the helping. No offense to you, but the only thing doctors do is administer other people's drugs. I want to be on the ground floor making those same drugs so we treat people with science, and not just by holding their hands."

"Your father and I don't hold people's hands. We take care of people properly, and do what we have to do to make sure they stay in the best health possible."

"I know, Mama, and I wasn't trying to put you two down. The world couldn't run without doctors, but there is a limit to what they can do. I want to reduce that limit and bring it down to nothing, so that eventually you'll have to come to people like me to see what we've come up, what science has come up with, because a doctor is only as good as the science behind him—"

"—Or her!"

"Of course, Mama! Or her! And I have a great surprise for you!"

"Don't tell me you're getting married?"

"Oh no, Mama, I didn't mean *that*!"

David glanced at his dad, "I've been offered a great viral research job!"

"Where?" both parents said together.

"The WHO in Geneva, Switzerland!"

"The WHO! That's fantastic!" said Papa. Mama did not look so happy,

"Now, don't get me wrong because I am very happy for you, David, but I was hoping you'd want to come home, to Hong Kong, or at least stay in the States, where I'm from. Didn't your advisor, Dr. Reinhardt want you to work for him, and be his grad student? That way you could always get your PhD from Stanford if you don't want to become a medical doctor."

"Now, come on, Sheri," said Papa, "he's just graduated and you're already talking to him about medical school or getting a PhD. I think it's wonderful he's been offered this opportunity."

"And Mama, I'll be able to learn, do some great viral research, and make a lot of money!"

"Of course, honey, you're absolutely right. I was just being selfish. I wanted you, we both wanted you here, in Hong Kong, near us, not over in Europe on the other side of the world!"

"And Stanford's not on the other side of the world?" said David.

"You got me there. Anyway, how was your summer job in Sarasota? Meet any nice American girls?" she added, coming over to give him a kiss.

"Or how about some nice Chinese girls?" asked Papa.

"I've met a few of both!" David laughed coyly and both parents smiled.

Then he turned serious, "I don't like the political situation here in Hong Kong: first, the Umbrella Revolution and now the pro-democracy student movement. Been going on for four years already. Why would I want to work here? Honestly, I fear for you guys all the time when you go to work. Right now, we're sitting up here in this penthouse and they're down there in the streets battling Beijing. The Chinese Communist Party thinks that because it took Hong Kong back from Britain, we citizens no longer have any rights."

"That was in 1997, David, the year after you were born," said Papa, "And Carrie Lam is just trying to maintain law and order. The CCP isn't so bad. They're trading with the whole world now. Sometimes I think they're capitalists!"

"I beg to differ, Papa, I know how you're attached to the mainland, but we don't want Hong Kong to develop into a Tiananmen, do we?"

"I think David's very tired after his long flight, aren't you son?" said Papa to Mama. "Sheri, I know David's a big boy of twenty-two now, but why don't you put him to bed so he can sleep?" Papa went over to David and gave him a hug,

"What do you think, son? Aren't you a little tired?"

"I guess I am, Papa, I'm not gonna lie."

"Go ahead then, son, sleep the sleep of the just!" said Sheri, and she got up to accompany him to his old room when David said,

"I better not sleep now, Papa, because otherwise I'll be up all night when it's daytime on the west coast. I think I'll go out and walk around a bit until dinner time. Then I'll go to bed early."

"All right, son, you do what's best, but remember, it's dangerous out there with all those hoodlums running about trying to spoil our way of life."

"I'll be careful, Papa. Thanks, Mama." And with that, David left.

"Papa" or Cheng Nò Lät in Chinese watched his son leave. He curled his lip in anger. *What were these professors and students teaching his boy at university? And Stanford had set him back at least $100,000 per year with all their fees. What! So he could learn to hate China, his native land, the land his people had always known and settle down in the lawless West of the USA?*

Or,˙ if he went to Switzerland, which side would he be on?

Cheng Nò Lät picked up his cell phone and sat down in his study and contemplated the blank wall for a little bit. Then he dialed a number,

"Yu Xi Chu? Cheng Nò Lät here. How's the weather over there?"

"Listen to Nò Lät! He wants to know how the weather is here in Wuhan! What a stupid question! How are you, my friend?"

"Not so well, Xi Chu, not so well."

"What's the matter?"

"It's my son, David. He just graduated from Stanford in Microbiology and wants to go to the WHO in Switzerland where he's been offered a job."

"The WHO is a great place and he must be very smart to have been offered a job there. But I see what you mean. You don't want him going there. I'll take care of that, Nò Lät. We own them, and I'll offer David a job he can't refuse. This happens all the time with these students. They go abroad and forget about China. Don't worry, Nò Lät, David sounds like a good kid. We'll put him to work here. I'll be in touch. Bye-bye."

"Thank you, Xi Chu."

***

David left his parents' penthouse and took the elevator from the 30th floor to the ground floor lobby. He was more frightened going down than he was going up; the ride was so fast, he felt he was about to jump into the Hong Kong harbor. Once down in the lobby, he removed his sweater, and left the too cold air-conditioned building.

A blast of hot humid air hit him as he opened the door to the street. He hadn't been aware of this before, but suddenly the roar of thousands of voices sounded like gunfire as he tried to make his way through the crowd of pro-democracy protesters.

He walked along for a few minutes when he suddenly became aware that two men were taking videos of him and, for some reason that David could not work out, they did not look like the other demonstrators.

CHAPTER FOUR – WUHAN DREAMING

Wuhan, China

David, dressed casually in a sports jacket, white sneakers and jeans, was escorted to his gigantic first-class suite by the head of the Wanda Reign Hotel and two lackeys carrying his small bag and laptop computer. "Welcome to Wuhan, David Cheng!" was written in large letters in English and Chinese on the sixty-five-inch television monitor over the background image of the Wuhan First Yangtze Bridge, the longest double suspension bridge in the world. Classic Chinese furniture contrasted with the most modern of high tech designed for David's all-expense paid, three-day, three-night stay. Yu Xi Chu had not only arranged for his personal driver to meet David at the Wuhan Tianhe International Airport, he had called the Wanda Reign hotel manager ahead to arrange for his friend's son's VIP reception. Cheng Nò Lät and Yu Xi Chu went way back to the time Yu Xi Chu was caught for embezzling state funds and Cheng Nò Lät had helped clear his name. Yu Xi Chu owed him his life, and would do anything for his good friend and his family.

***

David was kicking back on the bed with a glass of champagne and caviar when his cell phone rang and his mother and father crowded into his WhatsApp screen to find out how his two-hour flight had gone. They wanted to know whether he had been able to meet the manager of the hotel; and also when he was going to meet Mr. Tchao Suk Dong, the director of the Wuhan Institute of Virology in the Jiagxia District, *and* whether he was going to go out to a restaurant, *and* whether—.

"—Tomorrow, Mama, don't worry. I told you only four hours ago when I left. I'll see him at nine am tomorrow. I just got here! Bye."

"Don't hang up, David! And make sure you get a good night's sleep, David. You need your rest."

"And remember to keep your mind open, David," said Papa in Chinese, "an open mind is open to everything, especially in Wuhan!"

"Don't worry, Papa, it's true, I didn't want to come here but the place is beautiful, just like you said it was, and your friend Dr. Yu Xi Chu has arranged for everything. He was on the phone as soon as I arrived in the Tianhe airport. I felt like a king arriving here. He sent his chauffeur in his Bentley to meet me. You should see the chandeliers, the furniture, the views of that double suspension bridge, the city. The suite where I'm

at is almost as big as our apartment, without the view of
the harbor, of course! Don't worry, I'm ok, I'm doing
well. Bye Papa, bye Mama."

"All right, son, you listen to Yu Xi Chu, he
knows a lot and will steer you in the right direct—."

David clicked on the red and white *hang-up icon*
to end the call.

Director Tchao Suk Dong insisted the initial
meeting be held at the hotel as he did not want David to
come to the lab until he felt certain that David would be
joining the team.
And of course Dr. Tchao Suk Dong had chosen the
Wanda Reign; he knew from experience that their
breakfasts were particularly good.

Tchao Suk Dong liked his food. The son of a
Chinese father and Korean mother—and hence his
middle name, Suk, handed down from her—Tchao was
fifty-nine, short and fat. Never very athletic as a child, he
also wore thick glasses over fading yellow-brown eyes
set into an over-round face. Some people thought he
looked like the friendly father version of Kim Jong Un.
Unlike the North Korean dictator, Tchao was dressed in
a rumpled shapeless suit (it looked like it had been
bought in the local thrift store) and there was cigarette
ash on his lapel. Yes, Tchao Suk Dong was a chain
smoker, but he had a soft kindly expression, as if he
could be a mentor to someone. Would he become David

Cheng's mentor? He was only 5'2" and gazed up at the handsome Chinese American who was at least six feet and was ordering a large portion of waffles, eggs and bacon and a huge glass of orange juice. Achh! Tchao looked down at his own gut as he caught a glimpse of his reflection in the window. He didn't like what he saw. China was becoming like the US: two thirds of the Chinese people were overweight.

"These are quite good. You Americans eat these waffles now, right?"

"Do you see me as American, Sir? Only on my mother's side," said David.

"What I mean is you've been away four years so you know, you're American now! At Stanford! We send many of our students there. Excellent school for the basics. But you know, the Americans, they think they know everything but they're far behind in viral research."

"The Americans I know have told me that they do the best research in the world."

"What else can they say, David? They have no culture, no savoir-faire, no taste, but what they do have, the only thing they have, let's face it, is business. They love business and so viral research for them is a business. They have to make money. Non-stop, all the time. Research for humanity is for profit, not really for humanity, even though they call it that. Once you understand that everything is based on money in the

United States—that the only thing they care about is money—you can use the Americans for all the wonderful things they offer to this world. The difference between what we do and what they do is that they will throw money at a project only if the return will be very big. We throw big money into research but there are no strings attached to it. Maybe the research will bring fruit, but probably it won't."

"What is the major focus of your department, Dr. Tchao?" asked David.

Tchao knew this question was about to be posed, and was fully prepared to give the conventional answer. He always ensured the appropriate wording was used. He did not want to later be accused of misleading a prospective member of staff,

"Classified viral research-important work affecting the security of China is done in the Bio Safety lab in the Wuhan Virology Institute in the Jiagxia District," he said mechanically. "The Lab has been churning out major discoveries there since 1956. At my lab we have unlimited funds available and only man our facilities with the best workers around, people like yourself, for example, students who have attended top rate Western, and preferably US, institutions; who speak and read English, because, let's face it, most of the important work is done in English—but naturally, as we Chinese go about our lives, we hope to change that and dominate, yes, dominate—" Tchao Suk Dong checked himself. He needed to speak clearly and carefully,

"—One of the topics we are investigating is the process of cleavage of the entry protein. Once the virus has found an entry site to the cell, it needs to insert its RNA. We are investigating the potential cleavage sites and one of the possible methods could be furin protease. As you probably know the MERS-CoV contains a furin cleavage site. Not that we are especially interested in camel piss, of course, but it's an example, but S glycoprotein from Ugandan bats can bind to human cells without mediating virus entry, unless we spice it up with protease trypsin."

David's lips trembled slightly as he struggled to capture everything.

"I'm sorry, I was going on a bit there. David, listen to me. I always find that the greatest scientific minds are able to explain a complex subject in just a few simple words that the ordinary Chinaman in the factory or on a farm can immediately understand. So just imagine I am that ordinary Chinaman and you are trying to explain the importance of virology research. Go ahead."

"Well," David coughed into his fist as he tried to gain time to gather his thoughts, "You want me to talk?"

"Yes, please do."

David would have preferred to talk for an hour about R0, or R Nought, that the Americans called 'zero' or R zero. His mind flashed on serological and antigen tests for HIV, malaria and flu, mutations and many other features. He was aware that time was passing by.

His face formed a wide grimace as he tried to get his thoughts organized. He tried to recall the statistics but he was still unprepared. He should have known that he would have been asked these questions. What was the matter with him?

He would have to guess and hope the Director wouldn't notice. He began thusly, "Viruses are the world's worst enemy. They kill far more people than wars, earthquakes, hurricanes, and many other natural disasters put together." He hesitated a moment hoping that this was factually correct. Then, seeing no rebuttal, he continued, "No one can see them. They are tasteless, odorless and silent. They are an ubiquitous enemy, hidden inside our bodies, on our skin or hair. They can spread from species to species. Your dog might be carrying a germ which could one day kill you. You might think that in the summer the flu would have gone away, except it might still be lurking unnoticed in a relatively small number of people. And then, suddenly, the flu might burst into action again in October. For example, the Spanish Flu of 1918 to1919 did just that, and is said to have killed fifty million people around the world."

David hesitated, worrying that the fifty million number might not be correct. There was no signal of this on the Directors face, so he continued,

"As researchers we try to find vaccines—"

David stopped again, wondering if the word vaccine would be understood by the common man—
"*vaccines*, you know, a shot to stop you from getting the illness. But we have had very little success. We don't even know for sure who has a virus or who doesn't, or whether that person had it previously and had recovered, or whether they were even immune to start with."

David wanted to talk about antibody tests and compare them to T-cell tests but knew he would fail if he did and fortunately, Tchao interceded,

"Very good so far, but what about R values and exponential growth?"

David smiled as this was the easy part. He liked to play this game with non-virology students at Stanford. The math students always got it:

"Let's say I'm infected and during the first three days before I feel ill I infect two others. and they each infect two more. As anyone Chinese who likes to gamble—and I believe there are quite a few—will be able to calculate, after one month over one thousand will be infected; and one million after two months, one billion in three months, and the entire world's population in the following nine days! Fortunately, that is unlikely to ever happen as it becomes harder and harder to find new victims when so many people you come into contact with are already infected or subsequently immune."

David sat back in his chair waiting to see how he had scored.

But Tchao smiled, knowing that he was once again in control of the meeting.

"That was very good, David. Now, let's get down to business. First of all, I would very much like you to join our team. I think your place is with us. We have a lot to offer you. And you have a lot to offer us. If you decided to join us, you would be working with a small team of ten other top researchers. Now, I'm not a hypocrite because I believe money is very important. I know what the WHO will offer you as a salary. We are prepared to offer three times as much."

David was stunned by this declaration but not persuaded.

"Thank you very much. I am flattered by your offer, but I am inclined to say no since I believe I can save more lives by working at the WHO."

David surprised himself by rising from his chair and holding his hand out to say good-bye to Tchao.

The director remained seated. His jovial expression turned into a serious look that surprised David for a moment. Tchao bent across the table and whispered,

"David this is the most important decision you will ever make in your life. What I am about to tell you must never be repeated to anyone."

Looking around the room to ensure no one could hear him, the director grabbed David's forearm and made him sit down again. There was a fervor in his voice, and his eyes were sparkling,

"We believe we have discovered a virus which is one of the deadliest ever. We are desperately trying to find an effective vaccine *before* it spreads to humans! You can be part of our team and become that scientist, yes *that one*, to discover the vaccine to save humanity!"

Tchao's face relaxed as he removed his grip on David's arm. He sat back in his chair and found his composure. He knew he had struck a nerve,

"And David, I want you to please accept this gift for being so kind as to come all the way to smoggy Wuhan to meet me." The director searched in his jacket pocket for the gift, and handed it to him,

"Here I have the very latest Huawei smartphone."

"For me!" David was delighted. "Thank you so much, S——."

"But wait, there's more," the director continued, "It has an account which has been credited with $10,000 US which will expire in three days' time. You have until then complete freedom to spend the money—on anything and anywhere—you want."

Tchao arose from his chair as he summoned the waiter to bring him the breakfast check, "Oh, and if you want to join the team you should meet them first. Just call me on your new Huawei!"

CHAPTER FIVE – OBLIGATION OBLIGE

Back in the Wanda Reign Hotel, David Cheng looked up briefly from his new Huawei cellphone to stare blankly at other images flitting by on the sixty-five-inch TV screen. *A vaccine to save humanity!* That could be him, David Cheng! This was an incredible opportunity! And on top of it all, *if he wanted*, he could spend ten thousand dollars!

But hadn't he wanted to work in Switzerland at the WHO?

He could still see the face of Tchao Suk Dong smiling at him as he pulled out this new 5G Huawei from his pocket. Yes, besides the best job in the world and an expensive Smartphone, the director had offered little old him, David Cheng, ten grand to do whatever he wanted in the next seventy-two hours.

Three days to spend ten grand or the money would disappear! That was a weird deal but David was too caught up in the details to think too much about it.

He glanced down at his Huawei and his thumbs started worked overtime scanning screens, saving them, and then deleting them. *What could he possibly want that he didn't already have?* Just the phone itself was far more than he needed. It was a deep-sea blue, dual Sim card 5G Huawei with eight gigs of Ram and a memory of 256 gigs. Worth a good thousand dollars minimum!

His FaceTime screen suddenly buzzed with his parents hiding behind the electrons if only he pressed on the green answer icon. He wouldn't do it; he didn't want to talk to them. Not yet. Nor did he want to send them an automatic message to call back later. He just let the message ring on until they finally clicked off on their side. It was obvious that he should take the job, but he didn't want to be influenced by his parents.

David pressed on the "Notes" application of his regular smartphone and triggered speech recognition so he could dictate his wish list of things to buy, or not:

- One hundred volleyballs to be sent to his old Stanford classmates
- Send them sneakers
- A roomful of flowers to Mama; I will have to buy out the central Wuhan flower shop; they'll think I'm crazy
- A $5000 hand-made bicycle?
- Top of the line electric scooters?
- An afternoon at the Wuhan motor racecourse and drive a Ferrari!

His Huawei chirped. He put aside his other cellphone and stared at the deep-sea blue phone with its silver screen. It was Tchao Suk Dong. *What the hell did he want? He only gave me three days to spend ten grand!*

"Sorry David, change of plans," it read. "Word's come down that you need to spend the $10,000 within the next twenty-four hours, not seventy-two hours like we originally planned. Sorry about this but then it's only time, right? Tchao Suk Dong."

David thanked Director Tchao and immediately clicked on Interflora to send his mother several bouquets of beautiful flowers. Then he ordered a box of the finest Cuban cigars to send to his father. He ordered a top of the line electric scooter for himself. And finally, he went back to the last item on his list:

- "An afternoon at the Wuhan motor racecourse and drive a Ferrari!"

Within minutes, David was out the door and off to the races...except it was he who would be *driving* a Ferrari! At least, he hoped so.

The Wanda Reign Hotel reception committee arranged for David to take a taxi to the Wuhan racecourse, which was technically called the Wuhan Street Circuit. It was located around the Wuhan Sports Center, which was a large sports complex in the city. Talking to his taxi driver, David found out that the street circuit was used for the China Touring Car Championship or CTCC, an FIA grade 3 event, but there was nothing going on the day or for the upcoming week. Instead,

David could rent a fancy sports car if he wanted, and why not a Ferrari?

David tried to pay for his trip but the taxi driver told him it was free.

"Is everything free here!" David exclaimed.

"For you it is, Sir. I have my orders from the Wanda Reign Hotel, and welcome to Wuhan! *Have a nice day*!" he managed to say in English.

David wandered around the track and saw a few cars taking practice runs and driven by young men just like himself. He could see that the grounds people took a lot of care with their customers, from fitting them with special fireproof suits and safety helmets to showing them how the cars were to be driven. David had once driven a Ferrari in California, and from the moment one got used to the engine noise, they were the most maneuverable cars to drive.

In order to rent a car at the sports complex, David had to go through a training session. He first watched a detailed YouTube video in Chinese about how to drive a racing car. The man who had made the video, a former Chinese champion driver, was there to answer any extra questions David might have. While he was speaking, a dour-looking clerk brought out David's "Ferrari" contract that he needed to fill out for the rental. David had to show both his California and Hong Kong Driver's Licenses, and check the standard boxes for collateral damage, payment and insurance on his contract. The agreement was similar to American ones, so David checked off the boxes mechanically as the ex-racing car driver explained all the intricacies of a Ferrari.

"Did you check all the boxes?" said the Wuhan Sports Center clerk who placed his rental contract in a scanner.

"Yes, I did, thank you," said David.

"Ok, then, well, have a nice ride!" he said as he pressed the "Scan" key and the document ran through the machine.

David went online on his Huawei and noted that the CTCC was fourteen laps long, so he thought he would just try one lap and push his Ferrari as fast as it would go. He would only do this on the straightaways because he needed to be careful negotiating curves with such a powerful racing car.

After listening to all these preliminaries, David suited up in a red suit and white shirt, both adorned with the Ferrari logo. Here he was in China staring at the black prancing horse on its yellow background and listening to the low growl of the supersonic Ferrari engine! Before he took his turn in the *Ferrari California*, one of the instructors waved to David, pointing to "La Ferrari" and shouting,

"First come along as a passenger as I take this beauty to 200 mph in nine seconds!"

David could not resist as he gazed at the V12 electrically assisted, 950 hp 663-pound torque, 1.42 kilo monster. No sooner had he buckled up than the instructor hit the gas pedal. Three seconds later they were out of first gear at sixty mph; two seconds later at seventy-five mph, one second later at 100 mph and in fourth gear one second later they were at 125mph as the car shifted into fifth gear. The driver pushed it up to 200 mph before hitting the brakes and returned to the starting line.

David peeled himself out of the car, his knees shaking from the shock of the experience.

He took a five-minute break before returning to the California model that he was due to drive.

He put on an engine red helmet decorated with the colors of the Italian flag and the Ferrari horse, and settled down in the cockpit while his handlers made sure that everything checked out.

It was time!

David revved the engine and took off slowly around the course. He completed one complete lap to get used to it. Feeling very confident and enjoying this newfound thrill, he started the second lap by increasing his speed and accelerating out of the first turn to hit the straightaway. But he fast-tracked too soon and momentarily lost control of his vehicle, veering sharply to his left and right into an oncoming car badly driven by another "tourist" driver in a blue Lamborghini. The

Lambo suffered minor damage but David's spun around twice before it crashed into the guardrail.

David's handlers came sprinting out onto the side of the track making sure that David was ok. He appeared to be in shock but was only stunned. He looked around to witness the devastation he had wrought: the Ferrari was completely caved in on one side, the motor was pushed off its engine mounts and the rest of the chassis was dented and scraped. David undid his safety belt and slowly got out of the car. He rubbed his neck and shoulder where the belt had dug in and left a big red welt. He was fine but totally overwhelmed by what he had done!

Strangely enough, and unbeknownst to him, the two men that had taken pictures of him two days previously in Hong Kong had filmed the whole accident from the stands. One of them aimed a small remote at a telescopic camera that had been targeting David from the roof of a nearby apartment building. The camera receded into something that looked like a gutter spout.

The two unknown men had also recorded the accident on their cell phones. They pocketed these and walked away.

Half an hour later, David was back at the admissions desk staring at the same man that had accepted his rental form for the Ferrari. He was not smiling and grinning "have a nice ride!" like before.

Instead, he sat grim-faced, and punched a few keys on his computer to pull up David's contract.

"Are you ok now? Do you want me to call the ambulance?" said the clerk.

"I'm fine. Why?" answered David, wondering why a rental car clerk was worrying about his health.

"Because the damage to the vehicle was extensive," answered the clerk. "So I wanted to make sure you were ok first? That you hadn't suffered any broken bones?"

"Don't worry about me. What's the dollar amount of the damage?" said David like the true American he was not.

"Quite a bit. Unfortunately, you didn't check the collateral damage waiver box."

"What do you mean? I checked the boxes I was supposed to check, didn't I?"

"Depends on what you want?" said the mechanical answer from the dour-looking apparatchik of a man, "See here? The CDW box, the collateral damage waiver box, is unchecked. That means you didn't want it."

"I didn't notice. What does that mean?"

"That you owe 360,000 yuan."

"What! That's about $50,000!" said David. "Oh no!"

"I'm afraid so, Sir, I'm terribly sorry!"

"So am I. I can see why you were worried about my health!"

"I don't mean to joke, Sir."

"Papa? Mama?" David was staring into his cellphone. It was an hour later. His parents on his FaceTime feed were dead serious.

"What's wrong, Son? You look worried," said Cheng Nò Lät . He furrowed his brow as was his custom when things weren't going well.

"I really screwed up!" said David. He proceeded to tell them the whole story, how Tchao had given him the money to spend and how he hadn't wanted to bother them earlier even after they had called and he had ignored their call. And then he recounted how the seventy-two hours had become reduced to twenty-four hours and how, instead of spending $10,000 and enjoying himself, he had crashed the Ferrari and owed $50,000 and all because he hadn't checked the CDW or Collateral Damage Waiver box! *It was so stupid!*

"You can say that again!" said Papa unsympathetically as Mama slapped her husband on the shoulder,

"Don't speak to him like that, you mean man, he didn't do it on purpose!" Sheri scolded him, "and he got a wonderful research job!"

"Getting the job is wonderful, David, really good, boy, but I can't help you with $50,000! That's a lot of money!"

"Of course you can!" said Sheri. "You have that money and more! He'll make it back. With his education! As if he needed to!"

"Of course he needs to, and it's the principle of the whole thing, isn't it, David? You have to take responsibility for your actions. That's what I've always taught you, because if you don't-"

"I know, Papa, I'm going to turn into a big bad giant, right?" said David, his eyes red. "That's what you always taught me!"

"I love you, David, but you need to extricate yourself from this mess. And when you do, you'll feel so much better about yourself! I'm sorry, son, but congratulations on the job!"

Sheri could only nod sympathetically, a beta female submitting to the decision taken by her alpha male husband.

David clicked off and stared at the blank screen. He began to shake and sob uncontrollably.

An hour later after he had recomposed himself, David Cheng grabbed his Huawei smartphone and called Tchao Suk Dong,

"I'm terribly sorry, sir, but I—"

"Yes, I heard. They called me from the racecourse. Are you all right, David?"

"Yes, physically I'm perfect, but mentally, well mentally, I mean—"

"It's all right, David, it's just a Ferrari?"

"*Just a Ferrari!* What do you mean by that!"

"I'm joking, David, but what I mean, is that an inanimate object like a car is just that. It doesn't have feelings. Your human feelings are the most important. Your health is paramount. Don't beat yourself up about a car." *That wasn't just any old car*, Sir! David thought, but he said,

"I don't know how I'm going to pay for it, sir!" said David.

"That's it, David, you're not going to pay for it. You didn't know about the collateral damage waiver box. I wanted you to enjoy your experience and to be able to spend a little bit of money after all the years of hard studying you have done! You need to have a little fun in your life. I'm going to pay for this. All right? Just forget about it, ok?"

"Ok, thanks sir, I'm really sorry but I so appreciate your gesture. It's really kind of you!"

"Like I say, no problem, David, I will take care of the cost. Does that mean I will be seeing you tomorrow at the lab?"

"Oh, tomorrow? Of course, yes uh, sure sir."

"Excellent, oh, and by the way, do you have the address of the lab?"

"Yes sir."

"Good, but when you arrive—please be there at 8:30 am by the way—call me but be sure not to go into the reception area. Wait for me outside the main doors."

"Yes sir, outside, fine, ok. Good-bye, sir."

"See you tomorrow, David."

David put his cell phone in his pocket and fell down to his knees. Then he ran his hands through his hair and went to the bathroom. He stared at himself for a long time in the mirror. His eyes were looking very red."

CHAPTER SIX – WUHAN STYLE

He peeped out his curtain the next morning at a sunny fall day in downtown Wuhan. It was 7:15 am, just enough time to get washed and dressed and wolf down an American-style breakfast before walking to the Wuhan Institute of Virology. He was surprised he had slept as long as he had especially as he had had difficulty falling asleep after the disastrous crash on the racecourse yesterday. How had that happened? In any event, Director Tchao Suk Dong had not seemed too worried about his crashing a Ferrari. The first thing he asked him about was his health and how he was feeling! *He was feeling like an idiot*, that's how he was feeling! He had a small welt on his shoulder where the seatbelt had dug in but other than that he was feeling happy and optimistic about going to the lab.

He followed Google maps on his phone and arrived at precisely 8:20 am at a large square building where he could read in both Chinese and English letters, "Wuhan Institute of Virology." He pulled out his Huawei and called Director Tchao but no one answered so he left a message. Then, 8:25, 8:30, 8:35, 8:40 am came and went and there was no director. Normally, scientists are precise and early, not tardy. Finally, at 8:45 and seeing no one, David reasoned that Tchao must have forgotten that he was coming and walked into the reception area. A pretty receptionist eyed him curiously. David went up to her and asked for Director Tchao but she smiled and told him there was no one by that name in the building. Panicking, and thinking that he was at the wrong address, David went out again.

He looked around and saw no one when suddenly a black Range Rover pulled up. The darkened window lowered and a masked, sketchy-looking man wearing a face shield in the passenger seat told him to get in because they were going to see Director Tchao Suk Dong. David was hesitant at first, but did as he was told and sat in the back seat. The man driving was also wearing a mask and face shield.

"I thought I would be working back here in the Wuhan Institute of Virology," David said, but the men said nothing more and drove a half mile away to a non-descript concrete industrial building in the middle of a large industrial park. It had no windows, no entrance door, no name plate but just the street number 12563. There were steel gates at the side of the building and David noticed a CCTV camera that read the license plate on the Range Rover. The gates opened slowly to a parking lot in the rear. The masked men parked the Range

Rover, got out and the one he had talked to earlier held his door open for him,

"Follow us," he said and walked to the only door at the rear of the building. David now noticed that they were completely covered from head to toe with light blue gowns, a face shield covering a mask under it and zippered boots. They wore purple surgical gloves and opened the door with a magnetic card. Inside, there was another door with a movable iris scan machine. As the men were smaller than David and about the same height, they each went in turn to receive clearance. Finally, it was David's turn so they adjusted the iris scan up to meet his eyes, and all of David's personal information appeared on a large monitor inside the second door. David was surprised that they already knew so much about him but he didn't ask any questions and followed the men in.

Suddenly, Tchao Suk Dong appeared in street clothes, and waved the men away. They disappeared down another passageway without saying anything.

"Hello, David, welcome to our lab."

"Hello sir, I wasn't sure what to do because I didn't see you and I thought I would be working back there, half a mile away?"

"They weren't there on time?" Director Tchao seemed concerned.

"They pulled up in a Range Rover at 8:45. I got worried because I thought I was at the wrong address."

"You didn't go inside, did you?"

"Actually, I did because—"

"—I did tell you not to go inside, did I not?"

"Yes, but they didn't seem to know who you were."

Tchao Suk Dong seem to wince at this but he quickly smiled a broad smile and said,

"It's very important to follow strict orders when one works here. Those men didn't, and I'm going to have a word with them later. They should never have been late to pick you up outside. What time did you arrive?"

"8:20 sir."

"Well, of course, first day on the job. You're a very responsible individual, we know all about you, and they should have known you would be at least ten minutes early. If they had been doing their job properly, they would have been waiting at 8:15 am for you. They need correction, there's no doubt about that. Anyway, let me show you the lab."

David thought it strange how Tchao Suk Dong had pronounced the word *correction* but he followed the director as he ambled slowly through the hallways pointing at different things, people and stations,

"We have eighty thousand square feet here divided into ten separate labs." They stopped at a door with the number "6" on it,

"This is our *casual room*, what you Americans would call a 'den.'"

"I'm not American, sir, I'm from Hong Kong."

"Precisely. And therein lies the rub. You're really not Chinese, are you?"

"Is there a problem with my nationality, sir?"

"Oh no, no problem at all. I was just thinking out loud." Director Tchao now took on a theatrical bent as he spun around the room pointing at things,

"Now, this will be your new home."

Director Tchao pointed to a twelve-by-twelve-foot table and twelve chairs,

"There are eleven workstations and a twelve by ten kitchen in each room containing at least one fridge, a large freezer and a microwave oven. There are two screened areas with two cots, sofas and bean bags on the floor, and at the end of every room in this building, there is a secure area for handling viruses."

David followed the director into another lounge area where mostly young people between twenty and forty were socializing/living/playing/working? David was not sure what to call it.

"I'll leave you here. If anyone mentions the "sweatbox" to you, not to worry. I'll speak to you about that later," said Tchao looking around proudly, "In the meantime, you're a wonderful bunch of young adults. Get to know everyone this morning, and then I'll come fetch you and we'll meet for lunch." And with that, Director Tchao Suk Dong was out the door.

David stared in amazement at everyone around him. One fellow was throwing a tennis ball against a wall and catching it. Three girls were dancing to Beyoncé's "Put a ring on it." One of the girls suddenly stopped the music to speak quickly about a chemical reaction experiment they were doing and the girls ran off, presumably to perform the experiment. Another person was taking a snooze in a screened-off area. Another was playing one of those Indianapolis racetrack video machines to the roaring sounds of engines and squealing tires. David shuddered as these sounds brought back memories from the day before. Another was running on a treadmill and finally yet another man was sitting in a comfortable couch deep in thought and staring at the walls. He was sitting in the middle of scientific papers and would stare down at a laptop computer from time to time and hit a key.

David jumped as another young worker yelled out, "I've got it!" and ran to his computer to type in an algorithm. In response to this remark, other workers ran past David to their workstations and spoke into microphones apparently connected to the "sweatbox." Apparently, they were getting instructions on how to run the experiment. At least, that's what David thought because he saw two figures in another station speaking into a microphone and others of his "colleagues" responding by giving the 'thumbs up' sign.

David now noticed a huge window at the end of the room where the sun was shining through over a luxurious parkland. He walked over and looked through the window,

"Don't be fooled, David, it's an internet video cam," said a deep voice from behind belonging to a nerdy little man; the man raised a small remote control and clicked.

"Look anywhere you want," he said and clicked again, as different locations came up on a giant screen. Then, he clicked on another setting control and wind and sleet seemed to chase the sun and penetrate the room. Then more artificial rain, snow and sun. He gave the remote to David to play with,

"My name's Jiu Li Nät Aut. You are David Cheng, right? Director Tchao asked me to show you around."

"Pleased to meet you, Li Nät Aut."

"I went to Berkeley in California for my PhD in electrical engineering. Apparently, you were at Stanford?"

"Yes, I was, but way after you, I'm sure," said David. "Tell me, what's this sweatbox that Dr. Tchao was talking about?"

"You're very curious so soon on the job but I like that. We can't go in there but I can show it to you from the outside. Come with me."

There was a brief silence while they walked over to the lab; David was wondering about Jiu Li Nät Aut's "very curious" remark so he asked him,

"What processes do you use?"

"We use genetic, biochemical, biophysics and molecular engineering in synthesis, cleavage and folding to understand how to control viral infections," said Jiu Li Nät Aut.

"And what about biosecurity?" asked David.

"We have labs at various levels of biosafety containment broadly similar to the USA's Center of Disease Control classifications of BSL-1 through 4. At the highest levels this includes airflow systems, multiple containment rooms, sealed containers, positive pressure personnel suits, established protocols for all procedures, extensive personnel training, and high levels of security to control access to the facility," Jiu Li Nät Aut explained. David asked,

"I assume materials leaving the cabinet must be decontaminated by passing through an autoclave or a tank of disinfectant?"

"Yes," said Jiu, "and also the cabinets themselves are required to have seamless edges to allow for easy cleaning. They and all materials within must be free of sharp edges in order to reduce the risk of damage to the operatives' gloves."

Jiu pointed to six cylinders,

"Oxygen tanks. Be very careful. They can explode if they contain flammable material, and in the presence of pressurized pure oxygen there is not much that can't become flammable."

"I know," said David, "in the cryogenic oxygen tanks on Apollo 13, the wiring and insulation inside the tank was able to burn when ignited by a short circuit."

Jiu laughed, "This material wouldn't normally burn in open air, but under 1000 psi! Boom!"

David was excited by the people and the atmosphere in the lab and realized that his parents had been correct in sending him there. It seemed it was going to be much more fun than taking a job in the WHO in Switzerland.

A little while later, Jiu Li Nät Aut and David walked out of No. 6 and passed closed to someone, apparently coming from No. 8.

"Hi, I'm David," David held out his hand but the other technician ignored him. Jiu Li Nät Aut saw this and explained,

"Don't worry, David. It wasn't that he didn't like you. It is a strict rule here. We are never allowed to have any contact or conversation with anyone from the other nine labs.
I know it seems ridiculous in a research laboratory but it's for security. The Director will be filling you in on this later."

David looked back at the man and saw him disappear into Station No. 8. Just at that moment a woman appeared completely camouflaged in blue virus protection clothes, similar to what the drivers of the Range Rover were wearing. She seemed to stare briefly at David, change directions and then walk away.

CHAPTER SEVEN – FATHER KNOWS BEST

"So, how did it go today?"

It was Papa staring at him inscrutably, tele-transported onto his computer screen from half of China away in Hong Kong. David was sitting down with his wet hair slicked back in an armchair. He had just completed a two-mile run followed by a hot shower to unwind from his day.

"I'm not gonna lie. It was pretty good, Papa."

"How 'bout Director Tchao Suk Dong? How was he?"

"He's the perfect combination of firm and flexible," said David. "He hates it when people are late—"

"I hope you weren't late?" said Papa.

"No, not me. It was these two other guys who picked me up at the Wuhan Institute of Virology to take me to this other lab. He didn't seem too happy with them."

"But I thought you walked there? You mean, you're not employed at WIV?"

"No, I'm working at a private lab about half a mile away. The name on the contract is

Lab 12764, Research Institute of China."

"That's odd, David. I assume Yu Xi Chu checked them out before recommending you."

David waved an employment contract in front of the screen,

"I wanted to talk to you about my terms of employment. I have to sign this tomorrow at the lab. It calls for a three-year commitment leading to a contract extension or a three-month termination notice either side. What do you think?"

"How much are they paying you? More than the WHO in Geneva?"

"Much more. They're starting me off in the six figures, Papa, with six-month raises figured in if I do good work! And an apartment! Just the salary is seventy thousand yuan per month to start, almost $10,000 US. I'd be crazy not to take this job. What do you think?"

"Sounds terrific, son. Good thing you decided to stay local before you went galivanting off to Europe!"

"*Local*. We're not exactly in Hong Kong here. Of course, they want me to sign a Non-Disclosure Agreement tomorrow. But they didn't give me an advance copy."

"Well, I suppose that's to be expected, David. That's almost standard nowadays when you're an inventor or working in research."

"I think I can handle it, Papa, we were tutored on these kinds of agreements at Stanford."

"You know, son, China is the future now. It will far outlast the USA in a not too distant time. For us Chinese, Hong Kong has to accept the reality of this new world order. And you, my son, are going to be in on the ground floor!"

"What about the pro-democracy movement, Papa?" said David, suddenly realizing he was the same age as most of these demonstrators getting clubbed in the streets by the Chinese police.

"They're just a bunch of jobless agitators paid a fortune to demonstrate against the powers that be."

"Maybe..."

"*Maybe*, David? Probably."

Just then, Mama stuck her face into his screen,

"My baby! How do you like your new job?"

"I love it, Mama. My colleagues are very smart and they're really nice to me as well!"

The telephone rang in the room.

"In fact, I have to go now. They're taking me out for a drink so I can get my feet wet!"

"Whatever *that* means! Have a good time tonight," said Papa.

"But not too late!" said Mama.

David switched them off before they could say anything more and ran downstairs.

He couldn't believe it. His colleagues were all there in the hotel lobby. David stared in amazement at everyone around him. First off was Jiu Li Nät Aut. Then, the fellow with the tennis ball. The three girls dancing to Beyoncé's "Put a ring on it." The guy from the Indianapolis racetrack video. The man on the treadmill and even the intellectual with the scientific papers staring at his laptop. The group of "Wuhan Dreamers" were all there for him, David, to show him a good time because they were all colleagues and all for one, and one for all!

That evening, the streets were packed and the night was warm in September, the result of an extended Indian summer. It was early evening so they decided to go on a pub crawl. They followed each other on foot for several blocks starting at an Irish eatery and bar, a certain "O'Malley's," part of a great chain of Irish pubs. One could find traditional Irish fare as well as Chinese food and drink. Then they found an English pub, "The Wuhan Arms," an American bar and finally ended up in the local Starbuck's where his colleagues drank tea rather than coffee.

David noted three things. First, that his colleagues didn't drink too much. In fact, they drank water everywhere except in the first Irish pub where they all had beers or wine. Secondly, it seemed to him that someone was following him. He didn't notice any particular thing but just had this strange feeling that he was being followed. And thirdly, that his colleagues weren't hungrily looking for women. Or in the girls' case, for men, or whatever! He couldn't figure out the mating game in China, and pointed this out to Jiu Li Nät Aut,

"You know that in the States, after two hours going from bar to bar we would have all been hammered and looking for mates!" said David, also noting that it was only nine at night and that they had to be back at work in the morning at 8:30 am.

"I know, David, and you're just twenty-two and it's only your first day, so take it easy!"

"Tell me, Li Nät Aut, why do I have the impression I'm being followed?"

"You probably are. We all are, I think. There are cameras everywhere. This is China, David. There is always someone watching. Hopefully, you'll get used to it. I know we did. Will you excuse me a minute? I have to go to the bathroom."

Jiu Li Nät Aut went to the bar and looked back. David Cheng was looking around, especially at the women.

"Do you think he likes blonds?" said a sultry American voice beside him.

"I'm not sure," responded Jiu Li Nät Aut to a tall American sandy-haired blond woman standing beside him. She had been watching David and his group the whole time from the back seat of the bar.

"He hasn't had much of a chance until now," said Jiu Li Nät Aut, "He's only seen the straight black hair of Chinese girls. But Asian or white, I think he likes traditional women, well dressed and classy, and those who are tastefully made up."

"Thank you, I'll make a note of it."

And with that the tall blond girl disappeared.

CHAPTER EIGHT – THE CLOSER

David Cheng arrived by foot at precisely 8:15 am the next morning. The two gruff handlers that had been sent to fetch him the first day were nowhere to be seen. Instead, Director Tchao Suk Dong had sent a demure assistant, who bowed to David, led him in and quickly scurried away. The Director stood up from behind David's contract and came around the desk to shake David's hand,

"Welcome to the Wuhan Research Institute of China. Can't wait to have you aboard. Let's just look at your contract here and you'll be good to go. Please have a seat."

"Thank you, Sir."

"You'll note that you're being employed as a *senior* scientist, senior because of all the outstanding recommendations of your major advisor, Dr. Reinhardt. And accordingly, we will be granting you excellent accommodations, which we will talk about afterwards, transportation allowance and a car should you need one, full healthcare and of course, an excellent salary of seventy thousand yuan per month. Do you have any questions about the contract? It's fairly short and to the point but take your time."

"Thank you, Sir. Thank you for considering me." And David did take his time, going over each clause painstakingly until finally they were each able to sign the contract.

"Of course," Tchao Suk Dong said, "this contract will be null and void until and unless you sign the NDA or Non-Disclosure Agreement. And that's what I have prepared here."

David again went through the two-page contract clause by clause, initialing and checking where necessary. Until he reached the "National Secrets Clause" and flashed on language like, "penalty for disclosure of national secrets to anyone, ninety-nine years in jail."

"This is very scary, Director Tchao?" David asked.

"What? The 99-year lease!" the director joked, "Don't worry about that. That's nothing!"

"I wouldn't go that far, Sir!"

"You're not going to be a spy for America, are you?"

"No, of course not, Sir!"

"Well then, why worry about it!"

"I suppose, but then, why put it in there, and anyway, I don't like to sign contracts unless I can fully back them up and ninety-nine years is almost two lifetimes! Do you mind if I call my dad?"

"Of course not!" said the director, "Give him a call while I go to the bathroom!"

David watched the director step out. Then, David hit the "Call" icon on his smartphone. His dad picked up right away and listened as David explained the situation.

"Well," said Papa, "I agree it's a concern. You'd have to be super careful not to contravene that clause, but I wouldn't worry too much."

"Worry a little then, Papa?"

At this point, Tchao Suk Dong had finished his bathroom break and returned,

"I'll call you later, Papa, all right?" said David as he stuffed his cell phone in his pocket.   "So? What have you decided? Or what has *Papa* decided?" David remained silent and looked at the floor.

"I'm not sure," he said.

Tchao Suk Dong seemed to consider David for a moment. Then, he raised his cell phone to his ear,

"Send the accountant in," he spoke into his phone.

Within seconds a very pretty Chinese girl about twenty-one came waltzing in.

"Hello, David," she said in a very familiar way. David stood up and looked curiously at her.

"Please, sit down, David, I don't want to interrupt your meeting too long."

"I believe you two know each other?" said Tchao Suk Dong?

"Xi Di Wan?" said David, as he rose again to greet her with a kiss. "Xi Di Wan! What are you doing here?"

"I was going to ask you the same thing! Small world, no?"

She approached and put her arms around him as he went to give her the French *bise*, the double kiss on both cheeks. But it was almost too much as she held him close and wouldn't let go, especially as they had only met once briefly at the Stanford picnic.

The director coughed slightly to bring the long-lost acquaintances back to decorum so she said,

"Excuse us, Director Tchao, I haven't seen David since last spring. And David, are you going to work for us? Please, please sit down. Have you signed up yet? I work in Accounting."

"Xi Di Wan will be handling your salary and will help you find an apartment and car and anything else you need, won't you Di Wan?"

"It will be *my* great pleasure, Sir!" said Xi Di Wan.

"All we'll need is for David to sign our standard Non-Disclosure Agreement," said Tchao.

"Is that all?" said Xi Di Wan. "The little old NDA? That should be easy. Let me look at it to see if it's changed?"

She went slowly behind David and pushed her left breast onto his right shoulder and said, "Looks okay to me, don't you think, David? Just sign there." She picked up the pen and put it in his hand.

David sprung an immediate erection which he hoped would subside before he stood up and left the office.

He was stunned and showed it.

He also signed the NDA.

CHAPTER NINE – WUHAN REAL ESTATE

It was Saturday morning and David was feeling very good. He had cancelled his return trip back to Hong Kong since he now had a full-time job as an epidemiologist in Wuhan, China. And he was awaiting Xi Di Wan who was going to show him a few bachelor apartments in the area neighboring the lab. She had told him she would stop by his hotel at precisely 10:30 am in a black Jaguar. *And she would be dressed in black as well*, but he was not sure why she had supplied this information.

However, when she drove up, David had to mount in the back of her four-door, E-Pace Jaguar because the passenger seat contained a little woman of seventy-five who was engrossed in some private conversation with a friend.

"Hello, David," said Xi Di Wan, "this is my real estate agent Mi Tu Wau."

"Hello, Mi Tu Wau," said David, "pleased to meet you."

Mi Tu Wau appeared to have a neck problem—or possibly it was a hearing problem— for she barely acknowledged David and kept on talking with her friend,

"...Of course, dear...of course it was so much better before, everyone knows that..."

"Mi Tu Wau?" said Xi Di Wan, "David's back there; we're going to the first site now!"

"I know he's there," said Mi Tu Wau, interrupting her continual conversation with her friend, "We went to pick him up, didn't we?...Hold on, dear...Hello, David? Wherever you are, and you, Di Wan, watch where you're driving, will you, we're first going to the Hongshan Residential District, and then over to the Zhongnan Road Residence?...so anyway, dear, what was I saying? Oh yes, it was just so much better in the good old days under Mao, when people did what they were told,..." she kept blabbering on.

"I don't want to first go to Hongshan and then to Zhongnan, Mi Tu Wau, we need to show David the Luojia residence; it's got a great view and it's the closest to the lab and the Shuiguohu Tunnel!" Xi Di Wan cried out.

"...Hold on, dear...What did you say Xi Di Wan?"

"Mi Tu Wau, could you get off that phone for a moment and concentrate on the road?"

"What's the matter with you, Xi Di Wan! You've been here many times before! I'm trying to have a private conversation!" the old bag screamed back.

"Well, it doesn't seem too private to me. Would you mind calling her back later? Sorry," Xi Di Wan said, glancing back at David in exasperation. David smiled. Mi Tu Wau reminded him of his grandmother.

"...All right, dear, I'll call you back after I show this apartment..." Mi Tu Wau pressed a few times on her Huawei android phone to try and hang up but was having trouble,

"Ahh, shit!"

"Can I help you, Ma'am?" said David. He leaned over and pushed on the red "hang up" icon and Mi Tu Wau was enchanted.

"Thank you so much, young man, that was very kind of you!" she said.

"We're going to show him the best studio in Luojia, aren't we, Mi Tu Wau?" said Xi Di Wan.

"Absolutely! And guess what, we're there now."

The trio pulled up to a guard house next to a barrier for a gated community. The attendant seemed to know the two ladies but took a picture of David and air-dropped it to his computer. He then raised the gate and they parked in front of a modern, five-story building surrounded by flowers and curvy pathways set in the middle of a nature park and tall trees. Mi Tu Wau was all of a chatter, now that she had finished her phone call, and was pointing out everything there was to offer in the building and the garden.

They rode to the top floor in a large modern elevator and entered an open plan, north- facing condo with one bedroom, and a huge living area and kitchen. The walls were all picture windows and looked out on the Wuhan Research Institute of China directly to the north of them and the Donghu Ecological Tourism and Scenic Area slightly to the northeast. To the northwest, David could barely make out the Shahu Bridge, but the view was breathtaking. David had his mouth open in awe as he went from corner to corner to study the apartment and its various views.

"I hate to say it, but we might have hit pay dirt immediately" said the student, although one had to wonder how many apartments he had ever known in his life. Besides the one he grew up in?

Xi Di Wan was always a first step ahead of everyone else, so she said, "I know you wanted to call your friend back, Mi Tu Wau? Would you mind stepping out for a half hour in the lobby? That way you can have your private conversation. I think it's important that Mr. Cheng really feel himself living in this apartment as a solitary bachelor, and not with us three teenagers. Because that's what he is, aren't you, David? You're a bit of a teenager. As for you, Ma'am, I'll catch up with you in the hotel lobby or back at my office."

Mi Tu Wau was only too happy to go outside and call her friend back.

As soon as the old lady had left, her cellphone plugged to her ear, Xi Di Wan walked slowly to the bed and sat down facing David Cheng. She stared at him for a few seconds. Then she pulled up her black dress, pulled the crotch of her red panties to one side, and said,

"Fuck me."

CHAPTER TEN – TOXIC ISLAND

It was about one pm and three CAIC Z-10 military helicopters were descending through the clouds south of the Qiongzhou Strait down onto the smallest of islands—called Retention Island—off the province of Hainan in the southernmost province of the People's Republic of China (PRC). Approximately one thousand people lived on this small island, and they had a governor whose name was Wul Li Lät. He had his binoculars trained to the sky watching the helicopters land on the beach.

He had first been surprised that morning when the director of the Wuhan Research Institute of China, Tchao Suk Dong, called him out of the blue citing an order from the President of the PRC. Why would the director of the Wuhan Research Institute of China need to talk to the governor of a small island who knew nothing about public health? And then, three minutes after this phone call, premier Ho No So had called him relaying the same message, *that there had been an infectious outbreak on the island,* and that the WRIC was sending a squadron of health workers to isolate and tame the virus. Wul Li Lät immediately called his handlers to take him to the beachfront.

First he noticed the occupants of the helicopter armed with QBZ-03 rifles and completely clothed in protective, light blue, biowarfare outfits exit the first chopper. Why were they clutching those rifles? Only two hundred yards past them at sea was a 130-ton coastguard type 218 patrol boat armed with 14.5 mm machine guns laying buoys with "Quarantine" signs on them. Unlike the helicopters, it had obviously been there for some time. Finally, a man whom he had never met but only seen on television, Tchao Suk Dong, dismounted the second helicopter and was met by second-level attendants that Wul Li Lät had sent before him.

The attendants accompanied Director Tchao to Governor Wul. After a few niceties, Governor Wul said,

"But we haven't seen anyone ill. You're the first one who's talked to me about it."

"You will," answered Tchao Suk Dong. "This island has had a particularly deadly outbreak."

"But how do you know?" answered the governor.

"We know. A virulent strain has been discovered in one of our labs. Trust me. We need to give ten of your weakest inhabitants—I believe there are one thousand

and eight people living on this island, right?—an experimental vaccine against this new strain of flu. We will test everybody for their immune strength, of course, but we are really worried about the old fragile people amongst you. And besides," said Tchao laughing, "we wouldn't give these old people a vaccine by injection; only a treated cookie, and a sweet cookie at that!"

"But I've never heard of such a thing!" protested the governor.

With that, Tchao Suk Dong pulled out an official government proclamation signed by Ho No So stating that three bio-technicians would need to remain on the island for thirty days to perform daily tests of the entire population in order to monitor the spread of the disease.

"You have now," he said.

CHAPTER ELEVEN – NASTY

December 2018

"Again!"

"I gotta get back to work, Di Wan, but first I gotta go to the bathroom. What's the matter with you!"

"Before you go to the bathroom is the perfect time for another quickie; the pressure!" Di Wan cried out almost too loudly, so David put his hand over her mouth, but she had to have it and he was up to the task.

They were face to face in what was not more than a broom closet up against the wall in the restroom of a small Japanese sushi place right down from the WRIC. And in the middle of lunch hour! They heard some knocking on the door which just made David accelerate and finish the job. Xi Di Wan was in ecstasy; David pulled away, urinated, washed his hands and left. Xi Di Wan was right behind him but locked the door before anyone else could enter. She took her time cleaning up, re-doing her make-up and opening the door. A woman waiting in agony to relieve herself, swore at Xi Di Wan, pushed her out of the way, and slammed the door behind her. Xi Di Wan could have crippled this woman with what she knew of martial arts, but she just smiled and rejoined David at his table.

They usually didn't meet at this particular sushi place because it was too near the research lab and they might run into one of their colleagues. A relationship with another lab researcher was not permitted but one with someone like Xi who was in the completely separate Accounts & Administration department was possible. Still it would have been very embarrassing to run into Director Tchao and have to explain away their being in the restaurant together.

"It's been eleven weeks, Di Wan, and still no vaccine. I spend my whole day thinking—"

"And fucking me!" Xi squealed, almost a bit too loudly and too girly for David's liking.

"Shhhh," he whispered.

"And David, you're eating that too fast! You're going to get sick!" She looked around to see if anyone was looking at them. No one was. She ran her fingers along his beard. "You were incredible, a sex machine, 'take it to the bridge!'" she whispered in deference to the soul singer, James Brown.

"You're tiring me out, Di Wan."

"You can sleep anytime you want in your little cubby hole at the office. Director Tchao said you could.

He needs your brain power; I need your manpower! I don't like to go there too much because I'd be really tempted to bug you!" said Xi Di Wan mischievously.

The days rolled by. David had been working eleven weeks at the WRIC feverishly looking for new vaccines to help mankind. David's work was fascinating and he didn't notice whether it was sunny or raining outside. His work was his life, his joy, his reason for existing. He didn't realize how much of what he felt was actually determined by what he took for granted. For example, there was the perfectly air-conditioned lab with its choice of web cam displays behind the fake window frame, which would automatically create the perfect day. Then, there was the staff that would arrive and leave on a phased basis so that few people had any contact with people from other labs. And yet there was plenty of social contact between the members of his own team. David's Lab 6 staff arrived between 8:15 am and 8:30 and left between 6:15 and 6:30, Monday to Friday.

Anyone who wanted to sleep during part of the day was allowed to use one of the three cabins, each of which had a small bed without sheets. Each staff member kept his own sheets in a locker.

There were the comforts of home like the twelve-by ten-foot kitchen which had a microwave oven, a stove, fridge and freezer. These were restocked every morning before the team arrived with sushi, fruit, milk, soda, beer and pastries. The freezer stocked frozen meals.

David had gotten into the swing of things. Most of his time was spent on his computer, followed by physical games and exercise. He found running on the indoor track best for formulating creative ideas. He would come up with hypotheses for certain tests, write them down when he returned and finally test them out on his fellow team members. David was the ideas guy; that's why he had been hired. But his team players were equally skilled in finding fault with his ideas; it's not that they didn't like David—David was very popular—but that was their job.

One of the best at poking holes in his hypotheses, was Ya Tsing, a computer scientist from Beijing. Ya Tsing was a little smaller than David and a former chemistry major at the University of California, Berkeley. David found out he was also a top beach volleyball player. He found out when his team had a four on four volleyball game in the gym; Ya Tsing was often spiking balls down David's face. Ya Tsing was as intelligent in the workplace as he was on the volleyball court. He always saw the big picture, but was also able to find the little foible that didn't work.

David thought again about not having found a solution to the vaccine problem.

But that was not the only problem he had. There was also Xi Di Wan. It had been great fun to begin with. She had initiated him in the apartment he eventually rented—real estate agent Mi Tu Wau had never suspected anything—and would sometimes knock on his door at two am for sex. If they went out in the evening, she would often want sex in a public place. They would be sitting at dinner somewhere and she would get that nasty look in her eye. And then they would have to use the restroom. This was fun, but he never knew what she might come up with. For example, one night they were in a nightclub slow dancing when she felt the need, but when they got to the restroom, she pulled out a whip and struck him across the back,

"Now you know what the women in Afghanistan feel when their husbands are amorous."
And with that she would tear off her panties and implore David to screw her. David would oblige because her bizarre behavior excited him. But she was becoming more and more bizarre by the day as well as more sadistic. David suspected there was something wrong with her.

David knew he needed to end the relationship. But how was he going to do it?
Incredibly, the relationship had remained a secret at the lab as Xi was not a member of the lab team.

David decided to confide in Ya Tsing and ask his advice. He met him at the local Starbucks.

"Oh my God, David, you didn't? You thought Xi Di Wan was in accounts and administration? That's stupidity to the nth degree. Accounting is her cover. She actually works for Security."

"You're kidding me?"

"I kid you not, guy. You know she's a fourth-degree black belt, don't you? She's also a Krav Maga expert. You know that martial arts discipline the police practice to take people out? Do you also know she had an affair with a member of our team who disappeared?"

"Once again, you're kidding me?"

"I wish, David, because his body is probably floating in the Yangtze."

"He's dead?" David looked very worried.

"No. Now I am kidding you. But he *has* disappeared."

"Ya Tsing?"

"What, David?"

"I need a vacation."

CHAPTER TWELVE – THE GREAT WALL

January 2019

He was a tourist, and yet he wasn't. This schizoid feeling was what he was experiencing walking along the Great Wall of China with all the other tourists. He had only recently become a Chinese resident with a Chinese father and American mother. But he was not really Chinese because his mother was American, and he had lived a number of years in the US and gone to Stanford, but still, what was it? Was he feeling that *mixed-race feeling*, whatever that was?

What was it? *It* was a cold, sunny January day at the beginning of 2019, of that he was sure. Quite a bit of ice had accumulated along the sides of the Great Wall during the night, and there were snow flurries blowing about. David took a deep breath through his mouth and rounded his lips to expel a long stream of icy air. He hadn't experienced this much fresh air in a long time. He had worked hard throughout the Christmas holidays and had finally taken the short weekend break he had promised himself for so long. He had really needed to get away from Wuhan, so beautiful in one way, but such a pressure cooker in another. And when he looked down along the wall, he imagined all these worker bees toiling for over two thousand years to construct the whole five thousand miles of it, the same distance between New York City and Honolulu! He jutted his chin up at the majestic mountains on the right, and then shook with fear as he looked over the wall at the grass far below.

A group of old, boisterous Americans walked past him. It was obvious that they formed a tour group for they were all wearing red wool hats. All except the tour guide who was not old—probably in her mid-twenties—and was wearing a bright blue hat with a tassel that showed off her eyes. Her complexion was ruddy from the cold, and her eyes sparkled with the fun she was having. David was struck by how healthy she looked.

Then he realized she was not just a tour guide but was making a video for YouTube, and she was using only Americans who had come to China for the first time. It was a basic travel video and the girl was just using her smartphone. According to what David could surmise, *anytime was the best time to visit China* especially if one were talking about the Great Wall, and even in the middle of winter.

"If you're not scared of heights, lean over the wall but make sure you hold on! I'll zap you with the GoPro!" she cried out.

David was intrigued by her use of the word "zap" and stood there watching her. She seemed to feel his stare so she turned around.

"Excuse me, do you speak English?"

"It's one of my mother tongues," David replied.

"Wow, really!"

"Really."

"Well, listen, would you mind holding my GoPro so I can get my shot?"

"Sure, I'd love to. Are you making a YouTube video?" said David.

"Maybe?" she said saucily and smiled.

Her teeth were like Chiclets; a sun ray sparkled off them. Thank God he was wearing his sunglasses. And there was something about her voice. He had heard it somewhere before, but maybe it was just her accent...it sounded Californian.

"Okay, now just keep the GoPro aimed at me, ok?"

"Hey, what about me?" said an old geezer who was standing next to her. His wife was eyeing him carefully.

"You?" the girl said, "The USA!" And with that she grabbed the man and bent him over the wall with her and flashed her smile back at David.

"Get that?" she cried out to David.

"Got it. What's your name?"

"Bonnie. And "yours?"

"David."

"You wanna give me my husband back, "Bonnie?" said the geezer's wife.

"Now come on, Mrs. Wohlbeck," Bonnie answered the fat and frumpy Mrs. Geezer. "Your husband and I just made a great shot for YouTube, right?" Bonnie answered, looking back. It was almost as if she were speaking to David.

She brought Geezer back to Frumpy Wohlbeck and put their hands together. Geezer pulled away angrily, not because his wife had made a scene but rather because she was such a frump.

"Bonnie?" David whispered to her.

"Yes, David?"

"Are you going to do any more shots with that GoPro?"

"No, that's about it," she answered.

"Have you finished with the group? I'd like to talk to you."

"Go ahead, guys! Be right there," she said to her group. Then she walked up to David and took her GoPro back, "Thank you for helping me. What's up?"

"How about some coffee? There's a Starbuck's near the Great Wall?"

"Are you asking me out on a date?"

"No, just for coffee."

"I'm pretty busy. You know, I got this group, and—"

"Everyone's busy. I'd like you to have coffee with me."

"Or else?" She laughed suddenly. Her voice was like a set of bells that startled David.
He looked at her. She was just smiling at him. He was in love like he hadn't been for a while,

"Come on. Ditch these old farts and come with me," he suddenly shot out. He was surprised at his bravura.

They were seated opposite each other at the Great Wall Starbucks. David stared deeply into her eyes, listened to her deep melodious voice, became startled at her merry, bell-like laughter. There was something about her that he couldn't quite place,

"It's Friday. Spend the weekend with me."

"What did you just say, David? You just met me!"

"So?"

"So, it's a bit forward of you, don't you think?" she said, pretending to be a prude.

"That's what I'm saying. Sometimes I think it's better not to think too much."

"Is that your American or Chinese side talking to me now?" she wanted to know.

"I guess it's my American side, but that's what you are, right?" he wanted to know.
David slid his hand over to hers and held it an instant before she pulled it away.

"Look at you! I have to join my group now. Where're you staying? Are you here now or are you going back to Wuhan?"

David pulled out a lab business card from his pocket and wrote his hotel name on the back of it, "Dinner at eight?"

"Sure, I'll see you then. I gotta meet my group now for lunch."

They walked out and faced each other. David leaned over and kissed her on both cheeks. Neither noticed the drone high above them recording their every move.

CHAPTER THIRTEEN – ROUND TABLE MEETING NO. 1

It was that time.

Director Tchao Suk Dong was feeling pressure in his bladder, and seeing no gas station in sight, he pulled off the bleak snowy road onto the shoulder and triggered his warning lights. He consulted his Rolex; he had been driving for six hours give or take and was anxious to arrive at his destination, but first he needed to pee.

At first he tried to write his name on the snow with his urine but then admonished himself for being a "child." Then he became anxious wondering if the person with the binoculars in the passing helicopter above could zoom in on his artwork and hold something against him. So he peed over his name and looked out over the desolate "moonscape" he found himself in. There seemed to be craters everywhere surrounding the long sinuous road that stretched out in front for miles. He shook himself dry, zipped up, washed his hands in the snow, dried them on his pants, and got back in the car.

Fortunately, his GPS navigator indicated that a left turn was coming up in about one mile. Tchao took that turn and saw that the road would continue on straight for about three miles. He looked out over the white landscape disappearing at the horizon, the whole lying under a lead-grey sky. There were no buildings or signs anywhere, no exposed vegetation—man against nature—and just the crunch of his tires along the packed snow and ice.

Tchao Suk Dong pulled up near a low-rise concrete building. This immense cube in the snow was surrounded by a twenty-foot high electric fence with coils and coils of razor wire on top. Out of nowhere, it seemed, military jeeps with armed drivers appeared circulating outside the fence. Thirty drones hovered above the complex. The passing helicopter that had seen him urinate before passed over again, and then shot off somewhere else.

Under the watchful eyes of the sentries, Tchao drove to the gatehouse entrance, which was manned by four armed guards. Tchao pulled out his ID, exited the car, let himself be patted down and yielded his briefcase over to the scanner machine. Then he underwent a quick iris scan. The apparatchik manning the iris machine gave Tchao a card with the number "27" on it, and pointed to some small tents dispersed around the building where he was to park his car. But first, this guard stuck a plastic cover over his license plate.

Tchao parked and walked over to the pedestrian entrance to the building.

There he was met by a very pretty girl in a brown uniform who smiled with her eyes but not with her teeth. Tchao couldn't help staring at her two 44 Magnum pistols, which were almost as big as her breasts.

"Can I see your card, Sir?" she asked. Tchao nodded nervously as she signaled to another armed beauty who accompanied him into a big circular room with a domed ceiling. It seemed completely empty except for a massive circular table with numbered seats spaced out every six feet, making fifty in all. The light was dim in the room, contrasting greatly with the table lamps illuminating papers and documents placed at each seating. It was then that Tchao realized that the room wasn't empty, and that he was purposefully not able to see anyone's face because of the lighting. When the armed beauty pulled out his chair for him at "station #27" he then understood that the other twenty-nine seats were already occupied.

"My Gentlemen and one Lady," a short man with a hollow but tinny voice started, "thank you all for attending today. You collectively represent all our military and medical departments. You are purposefully being prevented from knowing who is in attendance. The subject we are about to discuss is a purely hypothetical one, and I am sure I don't need to remind anyone that it must never be spoken of outside this room.

Consequently, I will not have to remind anyone of the penalty for breaking these rules..."

Tchao Suk Dong nervously lowered his chin to try and swallow as he peered blindly into the obscurity of the room before looking back at the speaker.

CHAPTER FOURTEEN – THE CLEANERS IN THE SWEATBOX

April 2019

David was in zone 1, munching away on a broccoli and beef take-out lunch in the "casual" area of the lab. He was by himself today since most of his colleagues had gone out to eat. He was absent-mindedly watching two cleaners whom he could clearly see through the floor-to-ceiling-glass wall, getting undressed in the intermediate zone 2. They were preparing to enter the danger zone 3, the "sweatbox," so-called because of all the paraphernalia one had to put on just to go in there.

Each zone had air pumped out of it so that the air pressure inside was always lower than that outside. The exhaust air would go through a HEPA filter to prevent pathogens leaving. The air intake would also be filtered, and every entrance or exit had an air lock. David himself was in his street clothes, but if he had to go into zone 2 or 3, he would have to change into a bioprotective suit, just like these cleaners were doing.

And if he were doing very hazardous work, he would have to wear a positive pressure suit where air was pumped in via a filter and pumped out again through a one-way valve; he would have to hope that his plastic face panel wouldn't fog up. This would also depend on how his body reacted to the suit; of course, each zone would be air conditioned at exactly the right temperature.

He was watching them strip down to their underwear, put on their hazmat suits, don latex gloves and outer gloves which they then had to tape on to their get-ups. He started thinking about all the pressure on their skin from the suits, the allergic reactions they might have to the latex but how necessary it was to be properly protected when they entered zone 3 where the lethal viruses were. Then, his mind began to wander to that undergraduate course at Stanford he had taken on "Experiments and Contamination." The experiment was to have one's hands painted with fluorescent liquid and go about normal activity. At the end of the class, Dr. Reinhardt switched on an ultraviolet light and each student would have to come up to the front to show where he/she had touched or been touched. There were fluorescent traces everywhere, on people's faces, on the tabletops, on beakers and test tubes, on electric outlets and cords, but when this boyfriend and girlfriend couple came to the front, each had paw marks on their buttocks.

David started laughing alone to himself as he had laughed out loud with his classmates before.

Then he thought of his new girlfriend, Bonnie, with no suit on at all, just the suit Mother Nature had given her, and he began to get aroused. They had been dating for three months since they met in January, and had spent their first weekend together...platonically! But the weekend after, things changed and David found himself totally in love with his wild, crazy Bonnie.

Since that first meeting with Bonnie at the Great Wall, Xi Di Wan had faded into the background. It wasn't that he had fought with her but rather he only had so much time and preferred to spend it with Bonnie. And for some reason, Xi Di Wan had not contacted him either and kept away, so maybe she also was going through her personal story with someone else?

Suddenly, David's cell rang loudly and brought him out of his reverie. He looked at the LED display and saw "BONNIE" in capital letters; that's how he had listed her, in great big CAPS!

"I want to see where you grew up in Hong Kong, David," came her deep melodious voice through the speaker. "Can we spend the weekend there?" she asked.

"Sure, and you can meet my folks," David said, "Mama is very keen to see you. It's funny. I was just thinking about you!"

"I bet you were."

"Hold on!"

"David?"

"IDIOT!"

"David?"

"Hold on, Bonnie! I can't believe these two idiots!" David was wildly waving his arms at the two cleaners. They didn't notice him. They had just left the dangerous zone 3 through the air lock doors and moved into the intermediate zone 2. And now they were removing their face shields!

"Take your showers first!"

"David! What's going on? What showers?"

"This one cleaner, Hee So Sik, has a sore eye. I saw him yesterday. He told me about it, and he just removed his face shield and brushed his eye with the back of his glove. Can you believe this idiot?"

"David!"

"Take your showers first!" David again called out to them. They must have seen him waving because they put their face shields back on. This time David watched the other cleaner, a certain Mai Tiu Bee Sik, take the large cannister of disinfectant and totally disinfect Hee So Sik. Hee So Sik did the same to Mai Tiu Bee Sik.

"Hi, Bonnie, I'm back. I can't believe my co-workers. One of these days that fool Hee Bee Sik is going to get infected!"

CHAPTER FIFTEEN – HELL HATH NO FURY...

She opened her eyes slowly that morning even though light had been coming in earlier of late with the longer and longer spring days. She was lying alone, dressed only in black cotton panties on the left side of her gigantic California king bed—when she had lovers, they would sleep on the right—and staring out at the yellow Yangtze river below her veranda. Hers was a large but cozy *beaver dam* or *bachelorette* pad with the extended mirror on the ceiling, the open plan studio flowing from living— to dining— to bed— room in a matter of seconds.

But she was alone.

Not that she needed to be. She was a beautiful, highly paid catch with a top job in Security with the Wuhan Research Institute of China. She had no shortage of lovers and hence her oversized bed for her oversized libido. She gazed up at the mirror and took a good look at herself. She ran her fingers over her smooth skin, her

large taut breasts, her slim waist and hips, her thighs....
Usually she only looked up at the mirror when there was
a stallion riding her, and she could peep her head out to
see how she was reacting: Was she being passionate
enough? Was she sexy enough? They always were; they
could never get enough of her. However, today there was
just she...she so beautiful, watching herself! She alone.
And yet?

And yet she leaned over to her night table and
seized her computer. She clicked on "Security
Files/Wuhan Lab/Zone 1/Casual Workers/David
Cheng." Yes, that's who was missing. David Cheng. Mr.
Studly. He hadn't been around much lately and why was
that? *Word had it that he had a new squeeze.*

Xi Di Wan clicked her computer a few times to
annoy herself with the sight of this American squeeze of
his. Xi had seen her before, at the Great Wall leading a
bevy of fat American tourists; sitting hand in hand with
David at Starbucks; going up to his apartment that *she*
found!—no, she didn't want to look at that photo, and
skipped over it. After all, she was just Security, why did
she have to fall in love with her targets?

Xi clicked on other photos of David Cheng,
drone shots of David at Stanford, Siesta Key, in Hong
Kong.

Xi gazed up at the mirror again and watched
herself caress her nipples. She was feeling randy, and
she was far more beautiful than this American girl with

her ridiculous toothy smile. Why did all American girls smile that way, clenching their teeth together in a rictus spasm?

She thought back to their first meeting at Stanford? David had no idea he was being groomed but he was by far the best student she had had to evaluate. *If I hadn't seen him, he might have gone to the WTO, and then the WRIC would have lost out. What a naïve fool he was! He thought it was his father who got him the job at the lab but it was really Yu Xi Chu, but if it hadn't been for me....*

Xi Di Wan picked up a rubber ball that she used every day to squeeze and strengthen her fingers for her Krav Maga and Karate training sessions. Her fingers had to be very flexible and strong if she needed to pluck out an opponent's eyeballs.

Apparently her name is Bonnie and she's a YouTuber...a YouTubette? Xi laughed to herself, and took out a permanent marker and wrote "Bonnie" on a silly face on the ball and squeezed the 'eyes' of the ball as hard as she could. *How will I get rid of her? I got rid of that useless husband of mine, Mr. Xi, after three months, didn't I?*

Xi stabbed "Bonnie's face" on the ball with a letter opener, missing slightly and cutting herself in the process,

"Bitch!"

CHAPTER SIXTEEN – HONG SWEET KONG

April 2019

"You want to take me to Victoria's Peak?"

"We're talking Hong Kong now? It's *Victoria* Peak. Named after the Grand old Dame herself."

"Whatever, David, whatever you want it to be. I want to see where you grew up; I want to meet your parents; where you went to school; I want to meet your friends; I want to know all about David Cheng. I love you, babes!"

"And I love you, too, Bonnie, and it's only been three short months!" Sitting in their favorite corner in the local Starbucks not too far from the lab, they were holding hands and looking into each other's eyes.

"Bonnie!" came the shrill call in English from the Starbucks counter. "Double cappuccino, extra cream!"

"David!" a lower voice called out in Chinese, "Your latte is ready!"

"I guess they're profiling us," laughed Bonnie, "they speak to you in Chinese and to me in English!"

"And you understand both languages, don't you Bonnie? Did you study Chinese in university?"

"A little. But that's boring. Now why don't you talk to me about our next trip?" said Bonnie deviously, and then there was that little trill of a laugh of hers.

"It's funny. I never thought of Hong Kong as a tourist site. I was only a schoolboy there growing up. You know, sometimes the school would organize museum outings, concerts, cultural events for the kids, but now I think of it, there's the Victoria Harbour and Victoria Peak, of course, and then we'll take the Star Ferry across—it's only ten minutes—and take in the skyline, and then we'll go to the Temple Street Night Market and get drunk!"

"David, you're so bad! I love it!...."

***

"I love it!" said Bonnie to Cheng Nò Lät, David's father as she, Mrs. Cheng and David crossed over on the Star Ferry to the Kowloon side of Victoria Harbour while the Symphony of Lights dazzled and sparked their arrival. They disembarked the ferry with all the other tourists and made for the "Eyebar" in "Tsim Sha Tsui" where they each had their favorite cocktail and stared at the constant changing lights of the skyscrapers.

David had the feeling that his parents really liked Bonnie, his mother particularly because she was American; and her father also, because Bonnie was really friendly and exuberant. She reminded him of his own wife when they were young. And so, when they found themselves on Nathan Road—the Golden Mile—walking along under all the lights and places like the Sun Lok City Night Club and Yue Hwa, they felt young again.

They all ducked into a quiet, upscale Beijing style restaurant and sat down in a quiet corner so they could talk. Mr. Cheng had never met any girl that David was dating, let alone one his dark horse of a son would even dare introduce to his parents. She obviously was very important to David, and Mr. and Mrs. Cheng wanted to find out all about her. And Bonnie was also interested in finding out more about David and the type of family he was from. It worked both ways.

"...You realize the British sold us down the river?" Papa Cheng was saying, addressing himself particularly to Bonnie. They had just finished a copious meal of shark fin soup, Peking duck and abalone, and were now digesting it all with sherbet and tea. "It should only have been a real estate deal. We should have paid China a vast sum of money to extend the ninety-nine-year lease. Instead those bastards gave China millions of people, many of whom had fled China to begin with, and now they were back in the Chinese Communist Party."

"It was signed by Margaret Thatcher," Bonnie noted, and David was impressed with his girlfriend's knowledge.

"Exactly, and way before you were born," Cheng Nò Lät noted. Bonnie giggled her trill of a laugh. David's parents laughed too because her laugh was infectious. They found her *so* likeable.

"The British should have allowed the millions of British subjects living in Hong Kong to have moved to the UK if they wanted."

"And maybe encouraged them to move to the west, anywhere in the west," added Mama.

"But now we have to accept this reality," added Mr. Cheng. "We are part of China and China will soon be the most powerful country in the world."

"Now, *that's* where I disagree," said Mrs. Cheng, "the US will always be on top, but your father and I will always be arguing about this, no matter what the time, what the company..."

David and Bonnie were tired from their early morning plane ride and day of sightseeing. They didn't have much time to spend in Hong Kong, so they told David's parents they would meet them at home after a short walk through the boozy area of Lan Kwai Fong. They had to see Lan Kwai Fong because David's parents had fallen in love in the same area so many years before. Music blared out from the open bars inviting them to come in, but they just walked hand in hand, rubbing up against each other like a couple of kittens, walking, always walking.

"What about us?" Bonnie asked, projecting wildly into the future, "where would we live? Hong Kong, California? In the future? If we were to live in the US, I would only consider California, if you must know!"

"That leaves a lot of the country out!" David laughed, going along with her. "How many kids would you want?"

"Lots, David, lots! Let's go to bed."

It was only 10:30 pm at the Cheng Nò Lät residence when they returned and wanted to go to sleep. Mama declared, "Now I know you two are very fond of each other and so that's why I'm going to put you, Bonnie, in David's room. And you, my friend, will sleep on the sofa in Papa's study." They were so tired that they kissed Mama good-night and did what they were told.

But when the clock struck midnight, David's phone lit up with the message: "Aren't you coming over to my bed in your room?"

CHAPTER SEVENTEEN – ROUND TABLE MEETING NO. 2

May 2019

The CAIC-Z10 military helicopter whirred noisily through the air over the low-rise concrete cube set in the middle of "Nowhere," China, about a ninety-minute plane ride from Wuhan. The only difference was that "Nowhere" last time was a barren, crater-filled *moonscape* in the middle of February, and the concrete cube and its guards and twenty-foot-high razor fence stood out from everything else; now winter had given way to spring and there were trees around the compound, and the landscape was green.

Last time, Tchao Suk Dong had to navigate icy roads for six hours and couldn't even urinate without being observed by a helicopter. Plus, the horrible ride back. This time, he was *inside* the helicopter, in first-class comfort, and the "cube" seemed a lot less threatening than before.

But not to the CCP pilot who touched down loudly outside the compound. Military jeeps appeared and surrounded the landing site. Soldiers jumped out equipped with rocket propelled grenades (RPG's) and aimed them at the helicopter. They struggled against the wind churned up by the chopper blades and strained to keep their RPG's level. A loudspeaker told the CCP pilot to remain in the helicopter. Tchao Suk Dong was to exit the helicopter but keep his hands in the air. He was then ordered to walk away from the whirring blades and be patted down in front of a waiting Jeep which whisked him to the entrance of the concrete *cube*.

As before, Tchao yielded his briefcase over to the scanner machine. Then he underwent a quick iris scan. Another apparatchik manning the iris machine gave Tchao a card with the number "6" on it. Tchao looked at the number and frowned.

"Can I see your card, Sir?"

It was the same pretty girl from three months earlier who appeared; she was dressed in her brown uniform, but this time she was not smiling. Tchao Suk Dong nodded at her, showed his card #6, and stared again at the 44 Magnum pistols she wore on each hip.

A second armed beauty accompanied him through the same domed room with the huge circular table. Again, the light was very dim and contrasted greatly with the table lamps, which illuminated the papers and documents placed at each seating.

Why was he now number 6 when before he was number 27?

"My Gentlemen and one Lady," the chairman with the hollow but tinny voice started, "thank you all for attending today. You may be wondering why most of you have been assigned a different number from three months ago? This is because the numbering system is random..."

Tchao noticed that there were only nineteen other participants in the room with him this time. Previously, there were twenty-nine. *Does this mean that I am less or more important, or that the meeting has become more secret because there are fewer people here?* But Tchao had not come for this, and the chairman was speaking to him,

"...First of all, I would like to hear an important report from Number 6. Could you talk to us about Retention Island, and what you discovered there, Sir?" he said.

"Of course, Sir, it would be my pleasure," Tchao said, taking the remote control:

"All right. Here on the first slide we see that Retention Island is a very small island in the Southeast off Hainan, and the population is 1008. We infected ten individuals using our experimental "delivery by food" method . We used a simple cookie which contained an active virus. We are supremely proud of this innovation."

He paused dramatically, hoping for some acknowledgement, but the room was silent.

"Now, please study this second slide: A test conducted on the island after seventy-two hours showed a doubling of the cases to twenty, and this rate of increase continued until 703 cases were finally detected, at which point we believe the contagion had run its course due to herd immunity. As predicted from our models, we had 310 cases within the first eighteen days and the final 703 within the following six days.

On this third slide, I should point out that had we started with just one infected individual it would have taken an extra ten days for the infection cycle to complete giving a total time of just under one month.

Now observe the fourth slide which shows that if only one person is infected and does not come into contact with another or simply carries an insufficient viral load the process may fail."

Tchao peered into the obscurity; he could see no one clearly so he sat back in his seat and waited for questions. Somebody piped up:

"Thank you, Number 6. I have a moral question to ask you."

"Moral? Please go ahead." There was muted laughter in the room.

"Aren't we just killing our fellow citizens by doing these experiments?" he asked.

Tchao pretended to pause for the answer but he was completely prepared for this query,

"It is true that fourteen people died here, usually within five days of infection and several more are obviously likely to follow, but please keep in mind that this is "Retention Island," and like the name states, it is an island detention center for those requiring re-education."

There was a deafening silence that went on for ten seconds.

Hearing no other question, the chairman said, "Yes of course, Number 6, I believe everyone here understands this and would like to congratulate you and your team on a very fine job!"

The room burst into applause.

Tchao Suk Dong nodded slightly with a tight-lipped smile to the moving shadows under the table lamps.

CHAPTER EIGHTEEN – BALI HAI, MY LOVE

August 2019

"You got the keys?" said David to Bonnie as they were about to close their front door.

"And I got our passports, too. I'm so excited!"

David and Bonnie wheeled their bags to the elevator and pressed the down button.

"We're going to Bali Hai!" Bonnie jumped into David's arms.

"Not exactly, Bon'. That's on Hawaii's North Shore, in the US. We're going to Bali, Indonesia!"

They were staring out through the hall picture window over the Shuiguohu Tunnel and the Yangtze beyond. Yes, Bonnie and he had moved in together to the floor below in a similar Luojia residence to the one he had lived in before. Same view, same layout, different apartment number. For obvious reasons, David had wanted to move all on his own without the realtor services of Xi Di Wan. He just told her assistant in Accounting who discreetly changed the apartment number in his address file.

What he didn't know, however, was that Xi Di Wan knew all about his comings and goings, and was even spying on him when he jumped in a taxi with the "bitch"—as she called Bonnie—to leave for Bali. Xi Di Wan was very disappointed in losing a lover, but she wasn't going to take it out on David who was a very important researcher in the lab. David's involvement with Bonnie was personal to her, but normally her job in Accounts and Security was to always know what was going on.

In fact, she discovered that David and Bonnie had been living together for the past four months after an initial courtship of three months. Bonnie worked for a national tour company centered in Wuhan and had a lot of free time, but it was he, the workaholic David, who seemed more intent on pursuing Bonnie, than she on him. *He can do what he wants*, thought Xi, *but I'm not going to be made a fool of.*

* * *

About eight hours later, the loving couple touched down in the south of Bali at Denpasar, the capital of the beautiful Indonesian island. And only one hour after this they found themselves sipping margaritas and piña coladas and watching a magical sunset on Kuta Beach,

"God, I'm so happy I met you," said Bonnie in her deep, melodious voice, looking into the rapidly descending fireball over the horizon, which tinted

Bonnie's auburn brown hair various shades of red and orange.

"At first, I wasn't so sure about you, Bonnie. We spent our initial weekend in January like a couple of old farts—*platonically,* I'll have you recall—"

"Yeah, well I made up for it, didn't I?" said Bonnie, as she massaged the inside of his thighs with her toes.

And just like that, David was like a wild beast. He grabbed Bonnie by the hand and ran with her into their beach cottage which was right on the sand. They ripped off their clothes and jumped in the shower, their lust knowing no bounds as they literally screwed each other silly: in the shower, on the bed, on the desktop and finally on the floor as they laughed and laughed. And then they slept the "sleep of the just and good" under a mosquito net while the mild island Tradewinds cooled them off.

They had chosen Kuta Beach for the first part of their stay because they were both novice surfers and wanted to enjoy the constant supply of gentle waves at the end of the annual dry season. And that night, it was more of the same, with cocktails on the beach, dancing in a local bar and nightcaps in their room.

The third day and fourth days they played like kids at the Waterbom Bali park, visited the Pura Luhur Uluwatu Hindu Temple, shopped at Seminyak and on the fifth day, they visited the Ubud Monkey forest.

Bonnie looked like a native with a red ribbon in her hair, and a native pink sarong around her waist. She stood out because of her height, but the monkeys didn't seem to be afraid of her as they jumped all around, chattering and grabbing at things. She and David could not stop pointing and laughing at them, but the monkeys just pointed right back at them and pretended to laugh, covering their mouths and jumping up and down.

When suddenly Bonnie's cell phone rang, a monkey grabbed it but Bonnie wrested it from the animal's hand. When she looked at the identity of the caller, her face went pale, and she moved away from David and the jumping beasts to answer the call.

And from then on, it was like a black cloud had come over Bonnie. At first she was silent and sullen, no longer speaking to David unless being spoken to; her answers were terse or boring, or devoid of emotion of any kind. That night, there was absolutely no bedtime activity. Bonnie perfunctorily said good-night and then turned over on her side, stayed silent for a long time until she finally drifted off to sleep.

The next day, Bonnie remained silent all morning, and then was barely talkative. Since they were visiting the Tirta Empul heritage site, they could both co-exist in this outside world but for David it was not pleasant. He was aware that something had happened but wasn't sure what it was,

"You want to get some pizza tonight?" he asked.

"What are you trying to do? Make me fat?" she answered, and then went silent.

"Excuse me, have I said or done something wrong?" he said, "You've been like this now since yesterday at the Monkey Farm. We're supposed to be having fun here?"

"Aren't we?" she said, and then went silent again. David grabbed her by the arm and guided her away from all the other tourists,

"You want to tell me what's going on?" he said.

"You know, we really aren't suited for each other, are we?" she said.

"What!"

"You heard me. We have nothing in common."

"You mean we're having the time of our lives and suddenly, you get this phone call at the Monkey Farm!—"

"—it's the *Sacred Monkey Forest Sanctuary*!"

"Whatever. You get this phone call. Who called you? Is there someone else?"

"I'm sorry, David. I just, I mean, I don't know, but— No, there's nobody else."

"Good," sighed David. "Thank God, you had me worried there! Look, Bonnie, let's just get out of this heritage site; I think we're getting spooked by all the ghosts here, let's go to the beach and get some exercise. And then we'll talk about it. Deal?"

They went to Seminyak Beach and found themselves watching a volleyball game. Bonnie had still not yet said anything to David about the phone call the day before. Her spirits had seemed to lift slightly when they left Tirta Empul, but upon arrival at Seminyak, she turned listless again. David was wondering if something was medically wrong with her. Was there something missing from her diet? They had been living together for four months, but he had never seen her like this. He was going to find out who had been on that call, but he would do it his way, through silence, and let her finally come up with the goods *on her own time*.

Curiously, Bonnie seemed to take a lot of interest in the volleyball game they were watching. All David had noticed was that two extra-tall Australian tourists with very loud mouths were playing against different people, most of whom kept losing.

"Come on, let's take these two assholes on for $100?" Bonnie said suddenly.

"What!"

"I've been watching them and this is the scam. These two Aussie bozos don't play very well at first and then they call over their opponents to the net, they say a few words, and then they start a game. Their opponents win the first few points and then the Aussies call them back again. And then the game gets more serious and slowly but surely the Aussies play better and better. And then the Aussies win, and I just saw them pocket the other guys' $200!"

David was amazed. Bonnie hadn't spoken five continuous sentences for the past twenty-four hours,

"Are you sure? Can you play this game, Bonnie?"

"Can you? You told me you played volleyball at Stanford?"

"Yeah, I'll be fine. I also play with my colleagues at work at the Wuhan gym. But what about you?"

"Let's do it!" was all she said to David, and suddenly, she threw her red sarong on the sand. She marched up to the two Aussies as their vanquished opponents marched off,

"Can we play against you?" she said to the Down Under Duo.

"Well, certainly Mate. Love to. You blokes American and Chinese?"

"This here's David, and my name's Bonnie. And we're *both* American. Ready?"

"Well, look at this, John, said the other Aussie, she's raring to go!"

"And you are?" said David.

"Hi mate, my name's Rick and this is John. Let's try a little warm-up, ok?"

They began practicing and Bonnie didn't look like that strong a player, which made David wonder why she had put them in this position in the first place. She hadn't told him whether she was a good player or not, but she *had* implied it. And he had to admit she was getting everything back.

They played a few practice points, best to five, and the Aussies didn't look too good, but Bonnie had studied them before so she knew they played better than that. David and Bonnie lost this mini-warm-up match 3-2. What was more troubling was that Bonnie was responsible for all the lost points.

"How about we play for $200 and we play with our left arms only?" Rick said quietly in a horrible, low-class, nasal Australian whine.

"Make that $300, and you can play with any arm, and even with your cocks if you want to!" shouted Bonnie to the amusement of a few passers-by who gathered to watch. David was getting nervous. He had never seen Bonnie like this.

"'Ear that, John, we got a live one," said Rick.

They were to play one game, winner take all, to fifteen. For $300! Everyone seemed to get serious and play very well. David didn't miss a shot and kept his team in it, but when there were points to be won, Bonnie came up short. There were no smart Alec shots by the Aussies. Money was on the line; it was *money time* and as the cliché goes, money is not everything, it's the only thing.

After a short period of time it was already 10-5 for the Aussies. David was still playing very well, but Bonnie was struggling. Suddenly, it was her serve and she got three points just on her serve alone. Then David missed an easy spike and it was 11-8 for the Aussies. It was the first time David had not done the right thing and made an *unforced* error. Then it was two points for the girl and boy for every one point for the Aussies. Bonnie and David weren't making any mistakes. It was unbelievable! Suddenly, it was 14-13 for the Americans! Match point, but here Bonnie tried too hard, was too cute with a fake, and the Aussies spiked a ball down her throat without even excusing themselves! And then it went 15-14, 16-15, 17-16 for the Aussies who were about to win again...but they couldn't! Three three-hundred-dollar points in a row! And then it was 18-17 for the Americans, their second match point. David served and the Aussies who needed to win the point outright to get back to parity played Bonnie hard with a fake, but somehow, somehow, she managed to just scrape it up to David who popped up a very high sitter for her to spike, and Bonnie, who had not spiked a ball all game, jumped up off her sandy butt and spiked the most beautiful bullet into the open Aussie court. Game set and match, USA!

"Sorry "mates," couldn't resist that, oy, oy, oy!" Bonnie yelled sarcastically, to the applause of the onlookers. David approached and she jumped into his arms. Their fight was over, and the Aussies, who were about to sheepishly walk away, did the right thing and smacked three C-notes into Bonnie's hand.

"Congratulations, mate," Rick said to Bonnie, "we've been doing this three months now and no one's ever been able to beat us!"

"Well," Bonnie said, "Next time, pick on your own kind!"

Five minutes later, Bonnie and David were in the ocean cooling off. Bonnie was straddled across her lover's lap, and David was sporting a massive hard-on when he said,

"So? We friends again?"

"I'm very friendly, David. With benefits!"

"I know that spike," said David. "I saw it in Florida. Weren't you in Siesta Key last summer on the Gulf Coast? But then, maybe? Or were you blond?"

"Florida, David? Don't think so. Never been there," and with that she sucked on his lips and ground herself up against him.

CHAPTER NINETEEN – ROUND TABLE MEETING NO. 3

He could get used to this. Today, he was to be the chief speaker!

Tchao Suk Dong had taken the same CAIC-Z10 military helicopter with the same pilot to what he was now calling the "Cube" where he couldn't identify anyone just as they could not identify him.

After the security preliminaries—*couldn't they relax these requirements for a V.I.P like me?*—he turned around to find the identical armed beauty from last time accompany him through the same domed room with the huge circular table. And of course she was wearing her 44 Magnums over her uniform. There was nothing sexier than a tall woman in a brown uniform wearing guns. And he was excited and feeling good about himself because again—he had to pinch himself—he was the chief speaker! The Chairman had handed him the remote and had gone on for a few minutes about how wonderful he was. His number had gone up from number six last time to number five! He nodded to his colleagues hidden in the obscure shadows silhouetted by the bright table lamps illuminating the papers and documents at each seat.

Tchao Suk Dong aimed his remote at the center of the table. A massive video screen arose, forming a circle ten feet high and divided into five sections. This was so all the delegates seated around the circular table could see the same video at the same time.

He clicked the start button: Fully masked people in blue uniforms with purple surgical gloves and face guards were running about pell-mell in a military field hospital. Outside the emergency entrance, ambulances were pulling up three at a time. Orderlies and nurses, some of them not even wearing proper protective clothing were loading coughing and choking patients onto stretchers and looking for vacant hospital beds. These were filling up fast.

A man with his face mask fogging up, his chest heaving and his head twisted unnaturally to the side, was fighting for air.

"He's dying. Quick! Get the ventilator."

Another ventilator was wheeled up; there weren't many left and the stretchers were lined up outside.

"Soon there won't be enough."

"Shit, it's no use."

There was a sea of blue uniforms, masks, gloves and covered shoes, all running and walking in different directions.

The man's body was now convulsing; his face was thrashing from side to side. It was all the orderly could do to attach the ventilator. The orderly was worried about his own mask being yanked off as the dying man grasped for anything, anything to survive. Finally, the ventilator tube was in place, and the orderly backed off to watch.

The man's heart was failing him. He was literally being asphyxiated. Then, the monitor flatlined, and the orderly now began giving the dying patient a massive amount of cardiac massage. It seemed to last forever but it was only ninety seconds.

It was over.

The man was covered in a sheet and rushed out. Time to make way for the next one.

After nine minutes of these different scenes of death, Tchao clicked the remote and the giant screen folded into one round monolithic block and disappeared back into the table. Tchao was so moved he was trembling, and he was due to speak immediately!

"Gentleman, the experiment was a complete success!" he said, his voice breaking slightly and shaking. "If you recall from our previous meeting, we gave the ten inhabitants of Retention Island a massive viral load in those infected cookies. And all of them came down with something. For most of them—however not for these cases—it was just diarrhea!"

His fellow associates laughed, more out of nervousness than anything else.

"We have to accept that the effect on healthy young soldiers will be far less than these graphic portrayals. The main purpose is to create sufficient panic with the general public so that the government calls for a lockdown to stop the spread of the disease."

The Chairman intervened,

"Thank you, Number Five. That was excellent. The video notwithstanding, let me remind all you delegates here today that what we are discussing is purely hypothetical. Our illustrious Number Five has shown us what science can do. Now, let's hear what Number Twelve has to say."

Even though no one could see him, Number Twelve sat erect and pushed out his chest like his mother had taught him: *he was to make a speech!*

"Gentlemen, the beauty of this lockdown is that it will lead to economic collapse and general havoc. The enemy will have no vaccine!"

"Thank you, Number Twelve. Number Nineteen?" said the Chairman.

Number Nineteen was a pompous, jowly man of sixty with a crisp voice and nasty eyes, and very convinced of his own righteousness,

"The most important need will be to persuade the United Nations and of course the USA that we will be making a humanitarian move when we send in our troops to occupy the country and bring it directly under Chinese control." He coughed dramatically to not only underscore the consequence of his words but also his own importance,

"We, and only we of course, will have the vaccine."

"Thank you, Number Nineteen, excellent work." Nineteen's jowls puffed out like those of a blow fish.

"Number Five?" the Chairman was now asking Tchao Suk Dong, "Am I correct in assuming you will be able to manufacture appropriate quantities of live virus to be contained in the food stuff we normally export?"

"Yes, Mr. Chairman, we can, with no problem."

"Excellent. Lastly, when do you expect to have the essential vaccine? We will obviously need it in case any of our own people get accidentally infected."

"We are still working on that, Mr. Chairman. Remember, Sir, that it usually takes twelve to eighteen months to solve that problem."

"Thank you, Number Five. Number Eight over there?"

"Thank you, Mr. Chairman. If I could make a comment about Number Five's research?"

"Go ahead, Number Eight," said the Chairman.

"Number Five, Sir, thank you for taking my question? Sir, have any of your research teams worked with a virus from bats in Yunnan, namely Covid-19? What happens if one snips a furin cleavage site from another virus and pops it into a Covid-19 one?" Number Eight was a bit of a wise guy so he added,

"You could probably get US funding for that kind of thing, and that would help finance your lab!"

Tchao Suk Dong turned red in his obscurity as everyone broke out into raucous laughter. The Chairman himself could barely contain himself as he coughed out,

"As if we would divulge any of our precious work to the Americans!" and he broke into laughter again.

As the general laughter subsided, Tchao Suk Dong, who was seething inside at the implication that he was not in complete control of his experiments, said in a deadpan,

"As you probably know, Number Eight, we have confirmed that blocking the furin-mediated cleavage in the Ebola virus does not result in a reduction of viral replication, so the outcome is not assured. We continue to study furin inhibitors antiviral capability. I hope that answers your very good question, Number Eight?"

Number Eight's jowls shook as he harrumphed, "I am very obliged to you, Number Five," but he neither understood the answer, nor for that matter his own question, which had been given to him by a member of his department.

As for the Chairman, he only understood slightly more than Number Eight so he said, "Yes, we're all very much obliged to you, Number Five, and thank you so much for a most instructive and exhilarating meeting. Oh yes, and just one more question, Number Five?"

"Yes, Sir, I'm listening?" answered Tchao Suk Dong.

"How long would it take to infect, let's say—and this is only a hypothetical, you understand—a population of, uh, well, uh, twenty-three million?"

There was a short silence as Tchao quickly entered the figures into his calculator,

"Using the same modeling technique, Sir, about seventy-two to seventy-four days."

The room went even more silent than usual and then the Chairman said,

"Let us all give a big hand to Number Five, whose most valuable research has brought China to the pinnacle of greatness once again!"

The apparatchiks all broke into a chorus of applause and muffled "bravos" after which they all filed out.

Tchao Suk Dong waited a few minutes for his turn to leave the room. He couldn't describe it exactly, but the meeting hadn't turned out the way he wanted it to. He had had such high hopes when he walked in like a king next to his soldier queen wearing her 44 Magnums over her brown suit. And they had all given him a wonderful standing ovation. He had even heard the "bravos," muffled due to the gravity of the implications of his experiments.

He stood up and looked around the room and noticed that the lighting had changed somewhat. There were numerous alcoves on the walls which each contained a priceless Ming Vase or other museum artifact. *What were they doing here?*

Outside, Tchao Suk Dong took a deep breath of fresh air. He could see the blades of his waiting helicopter churning slowly in the distance as the pilot prepared for his return.

Another armed beauty pulled up in an electric golf cart. He looked at this driver and she smiled back at him. She drove him to his chopper, her breasts bouncing in rhythm to the rough terrain. At least he had her profile etched in his mind.

He stepped into the helicopter, nodded politely to the pilot, strapped himself in and stared out the side window at the Cube.

Yeah, right, a hypothetical? Twenty-three million! Those fuckers are really going to invade Taiwan. Isn't that why the number of delegates drops each time we have a meeting? Have they been thrown from an airplane like the generals used to do in Argentina during the 1970's?

He took a deep breath as if he were gasping for air. His mind raced. *Is my own life in danger? Even if they don't take out all those who worked on the bioweapon? What will happen to my wife and daughter? Suppose the invasion fails? They will be looking for war criminals.*

I'll have to check on my passport ASAP. First go to Switzerland. Check on my Swiss account. Then off to Vancouver. Still got that condo. It'll be a new life. Still got that condo, still...

CHAPTER TWENTY – CONFESSION

September 2019

   It was warm, Indian-summer warm in Wuhan as
David walked the final block to his Luojia residence.
There was a huge cherry tree in front that he loved to
look at as he returned from work. It had blossomed in
April when it was at its most beautiful, and it was the
first thing he saw after returning home. It was refreshing
for David to have this walk alone where he could unwind
from his very trying days. He swept his full door pass
over the several outside doors to his residence. First
there was the garden gate where the cherry tree was, and
which led to the terrace outside. Then, there was the
outside lobby and the inside lobby doors, then the
elevator and finally his own front door. When he finally
arrived in his sunny apartment, it was a picture view of
the Yangtze river that greeted him. Usually, but not
today, there was Bonnie jumping into his arms before
they would go running or into the pool.

   However, tonight Bonnie was the problem and
not the solution. Or rather a source of worry. He had

received a call earlier telling him that Bonnie needed to talk seriously to him about their relationship. Whenever an American woman needed to *talk about a relationship*, there was usually a problem. That was David's experience. Ever since she had received that call in the Monkey Garden or whatever it was called, things hadn't been the same between them. Sure, there had been the passionate kiss and make-up in the water and in the hotel room after their volleyball victory. But then again in the six-hour return flight from Bali and their first night back Bonnie had felt "tired" after their long trip and was not too affectionate.

The doorbell rang which was strange in that she always used her key, but everything had been strange since their return. For it had to be Bonnie; he couldn't think of anyone else that might ring the bell. He heard the lock click and there she was,

"Babes, I've been so worried!"

Bonnie bounced into his arms, hugging him extra hard as if he were about to disappear. Almost too hard, it seemed. David was suspicious.

"So worried about what, hon'?" she said, as if there were nothing wrong. But David was not stupid and very intuitive as well, "Babes, you called me at work to talk about our *relationship*? No one calls to talk about a relationship unless there's a problem with said relationship, am I right, or am I right? So spill the beans. What's going on?"

Bonnie pulled away from David and started pacing up and down, back and forth, going up to him as if she were going to say something, then backing away and turning her back on him, pausing, then returning and then moving away again.

"Out with it!" said an exasperated David.

She stopped, moved up to him and grabbed his hands. She took a deep breath.

"Ok, this is how it is. You know that I really do love you, don't you?"

"If you loved me, you wouldn't have to tell me you love me in this way. You would just *show* me that you do.

Bonnie started crying. "I'm showing you that I do. I'm trying to be as sincere as possible."

David put his arms around her and held her tight, "What's wrong?" She looked up to his face, welled up with tears and pulled away,

"It was all a lie, David! Do you hear me?"

"What was a lie?"

"Our relationship. Right from the start, when I first met you. Oh God, what am I doing!"

"Sit down!" David commanded, and she did as she was told, "Now, Bonnie, start from the beginning."

"Remember when you asked me about that spike? The winning spike? And whether I had been in Florida?"

"Yes," said David calmly.

"And I said I hadn't?"

"Uh huh."

"Well, I was lying. I was that girl Karen you knew, that blond? We were talking by your porch and I really liked you but, I couldn't, you see, because, basically, you were...it was an assignment."

"An assignment? What do you mean?"

"I work for the CIA. I actually speak fluent Mandarin but I pretend I don't."

"Just like you pretended not to know how to play volleyball too well until it counted?"
She smiled,

"Yeah, sort of like that. Anyway, we wanted to recruit you as an asset. We knew the Chinese were going to offer you a job at their lab. We needed an inside man. So we tracked you down to Stanford, to Hong Kong, to Siesta Key, to wherever you were. I could show you dozens of photos."

"Inside man for what?"

"David, you are working for a biowarfare developer. That corona virus you've been working on to find a vaccine for?"

"How did you know I was working on a corona virus?"

"The CIA, hon', we know everything. That corona is one deadly virus your lab created and intends to use. Millions will die!"

"A lie? I was just an 'inside man' to you? Our love affair, a lie! A work assignment!"

David's eyes were livid as he slowly walked to the door, opened it, walked out and slammed it shut.

"David? No, no, don't leave me, I fell in love with you but I was not supposed to! That's what I meant to say! You didn't hear everything I wanted to tell you! Come back, I love you! Please. Please! Please!"

But David had run down the stairs and hadn't heard the end of Bonnie/Karen's remark.

CHAPTER TWENTY-ONE – THAI ME DOWN

David ran down the stairs, through the gates of his residence, over the bridge and around the greater city of Wuhan. All he could think of was Bonnie/Karen and the life he knew. Yes, *knew* as in the past tense because it was all over now. Of that he was sure. He stared indifferently at plum blossoms lining the roadway and swung at one, knocking off its petals. He headed back to the Qingchuan bridge. He started counting the passing cars for no other reason than he didn't know what else to do. Then he left the bridge and the Yangtze river behind and started walking again, gradually moving closer to the downtown area and the Soho bar.

He hadn't planned to go to the Soho bar, but as he was moving in that direction, in the direction of people generally, he realized he needed solace, human solace. He walked into the Soho almost like a zombie, like the angry robot he had been when he left Bonnie/Karen at home by herself. Bonnie/Karen, Karen/Bonnie, BK, KB. Who the hell was she? He was feeling very sorry for himself.

David entered the darkened bar. A drone that had been hovering high over him dipped quickly to read the bar's name and then shot back up again.

There were very few people at the bar so David went to the end where he might have a maximum of one neighbor and plunked himself down.

"Whiskey," he said in English, as if he were a pissed-off John Wayne.

David had one, then two, then three whiskies in a row. Straight, no ice, and nothing in his stomach. An hour went by and he consumed some appetizers, then some more whiskey. More and more people came in and the bar started filling up. By this time, David was staring straight ahead, trying to appear straight, but feeling a little queasy and still ready to drink more. What he didn't realize was that he was really very drunk.

A tall beautiful Asian woman entered, checked a picture on her smartphone and looked around. When she spotted David, she walked over and took the seat next to him. She slid her left hand along his right thigh and gave it a little squeeze,

"Buy me a drink?"

He couldn't help but notice she was very pretty and that her cleavage was spilling out over the bar.

"You know what she, see, she wants?" David asked the bartender.

The bartender seized on the occasion when she was looking over her shoulder to mouth the word "hooker" to David in Chinese. David smiled and slurred,

"Whatever. Whatever...whatever she, she, wants."

The bartender showed her a bottle of tequila and she nodded imperiously. Then he poured mostly water into a very fancy glass with colored straws and ice cubes, small bits of fruit and only a tiny amount of tequila. She sipped her drink and nodded again at David who was now bent over, splayed out, with his chin on the bar,

"Where's he from?" she shook David who was about to fall asleep,

"Hey! Where are you from?" she yelled at David again.

"WOO-HA," groaned David loudly.

"Wuhan? You sound like you're from Hong Kong!"

"Hong Kong Fuck WOO-Ha, WOO-Ha!" David yelled, and a few people turned around, "And you?"

"Thailand. Bang-kok," said the hooker, "Bang-kok!"

"Bang-kok," repeated David, "that's a good idea, Bang-kok!"

"Let's do some selfies first!" said the lady from Bangkok, Thailand.

She grabbed David by the hair and hoisted up his head. She stuck hers next to his and flash, she did her first selfie. Then another from a different angle. Then she stuck her tongue in his ear and glanced nastily at her cell phone. Click! The flash, then the shot. David was completely passive and about to pass out when the hooker said,

"Kenny, give this man some miso soup. He'll feel better."

Kenny, the bartender, took a ladle to a big pot behind the bar and served David some miso soup with dumplings. With her left hand still clutching high up on David's thigh near his crotch, she gave David only three tablespoons of soup and pushed the bowl back to Kenny,

"Just enough to get him over to my place and bang the shit out of him!" she said delicately.

"How much is it going to cost?" David blubbered, spewing bits of soup onto the bar. The hooker threw some money on the counter, grabbed David's whole genital package and held him firm,

"Nothing. It will be my pleasure. And by the way, my name's Hu Shieh."

"Hoo-shee?"

Hu Shieh winked at barman Kenny and took David by the waist and led him out.

They stumbled down the stairs, onto the street and into a taxi. Hu Shieh barked out the directions to her hotel and pushed David into the back seat.

"You want to give me a kiss, Hu Shieh?" said David plaintively.

"I want to do a lot more than that, my sweet," said Hu Shieh as the taxi sped off quickly.

One half-mile later, the taxi careened to a stop in front of a cheap hotel with a red lantern in front. Hu Shieh threw the driver some money. They stumbled up the steps with David tripping over his own feet and Hu Shieh sustaining him from behind. When they arrived on the second-floor landing, Hu Shieh pulled David into a cheap room, completely painted in pink. There was the standard ceiling mirror, whips, chains, dildos, candles and rope placed strategically around the bed.

Hu Shieh pushed him gently and filmed him from behind falling onto a double bed. David took up the whole width of the bed with his arms and was looking very sleepy so Hu Shieh whipped off her top and bra, jumped on top of David, turned him over on his back and stuck her large breasts in his mouth.

"Suck them! Suck my nipples," she ordered. David did as he was told but his eyes were closing and Hu Shieh was filming every move she made with David. His eyes had completely closed, so she removed her skirt and panties and took a close-up shot of her own erect penis.

She checked once again to see if David was asleep and made a call on her cell phone,

"Mission accomplished," she whispered into the phone. "Do you want to come in?"

One minute later, Xi Di Wan walked in. She laughed at David snoring away, his mouth open, as Hu showed her the video,

"I think that American bitch will love to see this? What do you think?" Xi said to Hu.

"I don't know if she'll be able to watch all of it," Hu answered.

"I'm jealous of you. He's pretty hot, isn't he?" Xi said to Hu.

"Sizzling!" Hu hissed and parted her skirt to reveal her stand stiffer. Xi was impressed.

"Who's hotter, me or him?" Hu answered. David began to snore loudly.

Xi stared at the ladyboy for a minute and removed her telephone from her hand,

"Government business, here," Xi smiled, "You're definitely hotter," as she grasped Hu's erection with her left hand and drew Hu into her with her right hand,"

"You gave me what I want. Now, give me something else."

CHAPTER TWENTY-TWO – REUNITED, 'CUZ IT FEELS SO GOOD!

He was face down in a pool of spittle when he awoke. He tried to turn his head to the right but it was so painful, he didn't even move it. Instead, he raised himself off the bed until he reached an upright position facing the headboard. There were little plum blossoms etched on the pink headboard reminding him of the one he had kicked last night.

He opened his mouth and wiped a bit of spittle off that had stuck to it from the bed. It was disgusting; he hadn't even removed the dirty bed cover. He quickly ran to the bathroom to wash his face and take a piss. Still feeling dirty, he stripped off and took a very hot shower. He toweled off and put his dirty clothes back on.

Feeling somewhat less groggy but sporting a splitting migraine all the same, he looked about the room but saw no vestiges of what had happened the night before. Had he porked that hooker or had she porked him? He saw someone slip a bill under the door for the night's rent? Wtf, what was he supposed to do with that? He opened the door and looked out but it was only the hotel manager going about his morning rounds. They looked at each other but David closed the door in his face.

David waited till he left and then ran down the back stairway to the street. He needed to get some coffee and all he could think of was downing two Dunkin' glazed Donuts to get rid of his migraine, if there were any Dunkin's in Wuhan? Oh, and some aspirin as well. And Bonnie? What about Bonnie? Or was it Karen? It was 6:30 am. He needed to get back pronto and, and...

David didn't know where he was so he flagged a taxi and in no time was walking through the five gates to his apartment, into the elevator, along the landing and into the front door. It was slightly ajar, and sitting there, staring at him from the couch and looking forlorn was Bonnie. She rose slightly to greet him but sat back down as he rushed to the kitchen to down a glass of water, and then insert a capsule into the Nespresso maker and prepare some toast.

He brought his creation to the table, wolfed it down and stared at her for a long time.

"Who are you and why are you here if you're CIA?" he finally said.

"I love you."

"What! Who does? Bonnie? Karen? BK? KB?"

"I love you! You have to believe me, David. That was the last thing I said to you before you left but you were so mad, you were out the door and didn't hear me!"

"Who loves me? Bonnie or Karen? Who *are* you?"

"I didn't know who you were and I was given an assignment. Yes, you started as an assignment; that wasn't my fault. And think of it this way. If you hadn't been an assignment, I would never have met you. So I sat down with you at Siesta Key, and we played volleyball together, and sure, I played on the Bruins team for UCLA—we won our division—and I liked you but you were still an assignment. And then I saw you again at the wall in January, and yes, that meeting wasn't exactly by chance—the CIA has been following you for months—and then we spent the weekend together and there was no sex and you were so nice about it. I knew you wanted me, and I wanted you, but it was impossible for me because you were *still* an assignment! And I explained the situation to my bosses and told them that I wanted to go out with you, and they said they were against it because at some time, they would have to come and break us up, but if I agreed to leave you on demand, on their demand, then I could deal with you in any way I wanted and so no, no our relationship is not fake; it's totally real and sure, it's complicated because—"

"So this tourist business you do is a crock of shit?" David asked.

"It's a cover."

"Sure, CIA is always cover."

"Don't be cynical, David. Even CIA's are allowed to fall in love."

David sat there brooding for a long time, alternatively looking at her and then at the Yangtze river through the picture window. He had to resign himself to the fact that *she was CIA, and maybe she really did love him.*

"What's that thing you have there?"

Bonnie had been twisting what looked like a broken DVD in her hand. Over and over again, she had been bending the pieces back and forth from the time it had been delivered that morning to her door. She had dozed off on the couch waiting for David to return when she heard the noise of someone dropping it off at 4:30 am. Then, she played the DVD on her computer and witnessed David's night out from beginning to end; from the bartender in the Soho to the hooker and finally to the horrific site of the ladyboy's erection in Xi Di Wan's mouth. It had so distressed her she had destroyed the disc but then realized that CIA obviously had a copy of it back in Langley, Virginia.

"Somebody left a video of you and that hooker with a note saying, 'How do you like them apples, Bitch?' it was called. I guess the 'Bitch' is me. I saw what you were up to last night, so I destroyed the disc of your goings on with that hooker. If you were just an assignment, I wouldn't have done that. Don't you understand!! I wouldn't have broken this disc! I'm CIA!! I'm not supposed to destroy evidence, especially evidence of someone I love, but I love *you*! I love YOU!"

Bonnie started banging on the couch. Then she broke down crying.

David went quickly to her and put his arms around her. They remained like that for a long time. David stayed seated but pulled away from her and nodded. He understood. And he understood that he was in love, too, that they both loved each other and there was no going back to an earlier time when he really *was* "just an assignment." Then he spoke,

"You realize what this means, don't you?"

She nodded back, and responded to him, shyly at first, then kissing him and crying with joy and tears.

"Is your name Karen or Bonnie?"

"It's neither; it's actually Isabelle. But you can call me Bonnie. I was Bonnie when we fell in love," she smiled. "And I'm still your Bonnie."

She loved this man. And he loved her. But then she became serious again, and so did David,

"There's something else, David?"

"Uh oh, now what's the problem?" he said.

"Have you seen this?" she said, and opened her laptop. She hit a few keys and a round table meeting in Chinese came up with English subtitles on the bottom. The lighting was very poor.

"Do you know what this is? Do you recognize this guy?" she asked.

"It looks a Taiwanese soap actor, but why would he be in such a low-quality video?"

"You sure it looks like this soap actor?"

"Well, it also looks like Dr. Tchao Suk Dong, my boss."

"Exactly. This DVD is a fake, and the CIA financed this, but a real live meeting involving your director and other Chinese higher-ups did take place. Know anything about it, David?"

CHAPTER TWENTY-THREE – SUSPICION

"How are you today, David?"

"Pretty well, Sir. How are you doing?"

"I'm fine, thank you for asking. Listen, the reason I requested this pow-wow this morning was that you've been working on our vaccine problem for over ten months and it's time for your annual review. Does that sound about right?" Tchao Suk Dong said amiably relaxing back in his chair as if he were about to be brought a big cup of hot chocolate and cake. He was hoping his relaxed manner would rub off on David who seemed to be particularly tense.

"Oh, most definitely, Sir? Don't keep me in suspense. How am I doing?"

"That's easy to answer. You're doing very well. A great job! And for someone so young. You're remarkable."

"Well, thank you, Sir. That's very kind of you to say," said David, only slightly easing up, "I try to do my best."

"And your best is outstanding! So tell me, where are you in the whole vaccine picture?" Tchao Suk Dong said, his eyes narrowing even more than their usual narrow selves.

"Here's the story, Sir. We're continuing to study furin inhibitors antiviral capability, but we haven't performed any clinical trials," said David, watching his director closely.

"That all? That's easy. I suggest you do some."

Tchao pulled out a special grant form and signed the bottom of it. "There you go. We'll need to fill this out and submit it to the state, but basically I just authorized your expenditures."

"Just like that?" said David.

"Just like that. Exactly, you have authorization" responded the director.

Tchao then pulled out a yellow legal pad from his desk and made a note on it,

"Have you tried other traditional Chinese remedies which we can isolate in a lab?"

"Yes Sir," said David, "although I must admit I *was* very skeptical of using just any drug, but then the others suggested we try Baicalein (5,6,7-trihydroxyflavone) the flavone, from the roots of Huang Qin. Unfortunately, we didn't have any success."

"Well, you know what they say? If at first you don't succeed... There are some other plant sources such as Oroxylum Indicum which is Indian trump. Do you know of it?"

"We haven't tried it yet, Sir, but we will definitely get on to it. I'll go talk to Jiu Li Nät Aut about it right away. Anything else, Sir?"

Tchao Suk Dong thought for a bit and shook his head. Then he stood up to end the short meeting, but David remained seated as if he wanted to breach protocol. This was an uncomfortable situation where the director was standing looking down on David who was seated and looking down at his feet. The director eased back down to the edge of his chair,

"Is there something wrong, David?"

David remained silent for at least five seconds, an eternity in this type of situation.

"Sir, you know how grateful I am to you for giving me a job and how much I love my work here?"

"Yes, David?" Tchao Suk Dong mumbled, leaning in towards David, not quite sure where this conversation was going.

"To be blunt, Sir," said David, "I *am* worried about something."

Tchao frowned slightly and murmured, "Go on, David."

"Well, Sir, it's just that none of us really knows what's going on in the other nine labs."

"Of course, David. That is how it always is. You knew that. I mean, I made that clear from the start."

"Right sir, but – "

"Yes? But what, David?"

"Sir? I know this will sound ridiculous, but someone has suggested that some teams here are working on, on – "

"On what? Spit it out, man!"

"Bioweapons, Sir!" David said a little louder than he wanted to, "Bioweapons!" he whispered.

Director Tchao Suk Dong sat back in his chair and sported a big smile. But if one looked closely, it was more of a rictus spasm a la Joker in Batman. His eyes were like slits, just as his neck muscles pulled taut. Of course, David was too terrified to look the director in the face so he didn't notice this.

"Bioweapons," Tchao harrumphed good-naturedly, "How ridiculous! Look David, I have never done this before, but this morning I will arrange for you to inspect all the other labs and talk to the different teams. Maybe you all need to better communicate and coordinate together. In fact, I would like to thank you for bringing this to my attention. Leave it to me. Now, go on, and get back to doing your excellent work. I didn't know you Americans were so inclined to engage in conspiracy theories!"

Tchao Suk Dong now rose from his chair as did David. The director bowed slightly as David left the office.

"*Bioweapons!*" Tchao chuckled to himself, "*Bioweapons!*"

Tchao Suk Dong was alone. He felt an urgent need to go to the bathroom, but instead returned to his chair and picked up his cell phone,

"Your suspicions were right. You'd better come in. We need to decide immediately on our next move."

CHAPTER TWENTY-FOUR – CRACKING THE CODE

"The director was here real early this morning," said Ya Tsing as David walked into the lab, "I think he was surprised to see me here so early."

David removed his raincoat and left his open umbrella in the entrance to dry. He wiped some water from his face and, looking at his watch said,

"Any reason he was here. I'm not late."

"He said he wanted to know how we were doing with our research. And that he'd be back late morning when you were here. Let's sit down, have a chat in that private office?"

What was going on! What was Tchao doing here? And why did Ya Tsing come in early? David could feel something but wasn't sure what it was. Then there was the hooker that Bonnie didn't want to talk about. Apparently there was something funny about her, too. But Bonnie had destroyed the DVD. And then that discussion with Director Tchao and how he had laughed off the whole bioweapons idea. Why hadn't Tchao gotten angry when he heard that story? He'd laughed it off! Tchao Suk Dong wasn't exactly the world's funniest guy.

Ya Tsing sat across from the table and looked earnestly at him,

"We had an interesting result earlier when we replaced a single amino acid in the S protein to create a secombinant PEDV-S with an artificial furin protease cleavage which was trypsin independent."

What language was Ya Tsing speaking?

"David, I think O-linked glycans are another hot issue. What do you think?"

"Huh?"

"David? David? What's going on? Are you listening to me?"

"I don't know, Ya Tsing, there's a lot going on. I can't really think about any of this right now."

"What's the matter? Are you sick?"

"Do you ever wonder what goes on in the other nine labs here?"

"Of course we all do, but - ?"

"But what?"

Ya Tsing motioned to David to lean in and whispered,

"Director Tchao had to take a crap this morning."

David burst out laughing,

"And that's what you brought me in here to talk about! How do you know? Or did he tell you personally? Is he going to tell you every day when he takes a crap?"

Ya Tsing didn't smile or laugh.

"The reason I'm telling you this is he used our bathroom this morning for his crap. After he left, he told me he'd be back late morning and that he had some urgent business to do. Anyway, it so happened I needed to use the bathroom, too, but when I went in there, I found a wallet. I figured it was his but I looked inside to check his name and I found this."

Ya Tsing pulled out a piece of paper from his pocket,

"This paper is a copy of his password code in his wallet which of course I returned to his assistant and came back."

"The wallet, I hope?"

"Yes, David, the wallet. So, this password - "

"I see it's in code, obviously."

"Exactly, but as you know, David, one of my pastimes is cracking password codes!"

"And did you? You say he came here early this morning?"

"Yes, and that's where you come in. I need your help. I have the whole code except for the final digit. I have it narrowed down to 1, 3, 7 or 8."

"Those are pretty good odds, Ya Tsing, but if we don't get in on the first three tries, an alarm will go off."

"Exactly. Do you want to take the risk of breaking this passcode?"

"What's the risk, Ya Tsing?"

"Our jobs."

This was a special chance to find something out. Almost as if this meeting had happened on purpose: the fact that Tchao had taken a crap in our bathroom; that the wallet had fallen out; the meeting yesterday, that whole thing with Bonnie...

"Let's do it," said David, "maybe we'll get lucky on the first try, a one in four chance. Let's try "3" first." No luck.

"Let's try lucky "7" in the US," said Ya Tsing. "A 1-in-3 chance?" No luck.

"Only one chance left, and a fifty-fifty chance of getting it right," said David. "I think we have to go with lucky "8" in China. What do you think?"

Ya Tsing looked hard at him, "We're risking our jobs."

"True, but we have to know, don't we?" said David. "We can't leave it there."

David raised his finger to tap "8."

"Wait, David. Tchao Suk Dong would have thought of that. That if ever his password was hacked, the person would go with lucky "8". Let's try "1" instead."

He clicked on "1".

A big banner appeared in black: "Access permitted."

David and Ya Tsing each had big sweat marks along their armpits. All of a sudden they were raking through reels and reels of files. Secret stuff, stuff they had never heard Tchao talk about. A whole new world. David glanced at his watch. He didn't want to have Tchao come in and find them raking through his files.

He focused on finding the file he hoped he would never find. His fingers were flying over the keyboard but then, there it was!

"Oh no! Oh please, don't make it be true! This is not happening."

Ya Tsing pushed him aside. Stared at the screen, "We need to find new jobs, David."

David looked off in the distance, and then at Ya Tsing,

"We need to do far more than that!"

CHAPTER TWENTY-FIVE – GOD BLESS THE CHILD

Tchao Suk Dong heard a knock on the door and sat up straight. He slouched a lot but only in private; image was everything and he always had to appear to be in charge. He was the boss, after all!

"Come in, Di Wan. Have a seat."

Xi Di Wan was looking particularly beautiful these days. She couldn't get enough of the ladyboy who would visit her regularly, and she had another lover on the side to make her forget David. As a result, her skin and hair were glowing,

"Well, look at you," said Tchao, "I've never seen you look so good."

Tchao Suk Dong was pacing up and down in his office, stopping alternatively to look outside or stare at Xi Di Wan.

"I can't say the same for you, if you don't mind my being frank," said Xi, laughing and tossing back her shiny black hair. "What's the matter? I haven't seen you like this since –"

"Yes, you've guessed it, it's the same problem again."

"Shit!" Tchao Suk Dong looked sternly at her.

"Please excuse my language," said Xi.

"No, 'shit' is precisely the correct word. We'll all be in the shit if we don't take care of this problem!" said Tchao.

Xi remained relaxed, but her eyes narrowed slightly in anticipation. She was Tchao's "closer," after all, his problem solver. "Bring it on!" was her motto,

"Where is the leak?" she said.

"You mean 'who' is the leak?" answered Tchao.

"Alright, *who* is the leak?"

Tchao Suk Dong punched his hand,

"David Cheng."

Xi Di Wan felt weak in the knees. Fortunately, she was sitting. She had lost her normal composure but soon recovered,

"What a pity!" she said dryly.

"Dammit!" added Tchao, "Why did it have to be him? He was such a nice guy. How am I going to find a replacement for him in such a short time? Where is the justice? Why aren't my picks justified? China is the future, everyone knows that, our one-hundred-year marathon for world domination. We will be the best. China is our future! Nobody can come between us and our needs. They want a vaccine! Everyone wants a vaccine. They have no idea what it takes, what I have to get through, what we all have to go through, to comb through the entire world's research. The fuckers! Now I have to get rid of one of my best men! Oh, Di Wan, excuse my bad language again, I just – "

"Don't worry, Director! I will take care of the David Cheng problem, and I know you will succeed in finding a replacement!" said Xi Di Wan, grandiloquently. Underneath, she had a very good idea how she was going to deal with David Cheng. It would be a very pleasurable experience she thought as she crossed her legs twice to relieve tension.

Xi stood up and walked over to Tchau Suk Dong who was several inches shorter than she. She put her arms around the slimy, fifty-nine-year old and kissed him on the forehead.

"Don't worry, Father, your little girl will always be here for you."

CHAPTER TWENTY-SIX – VOLLEYBALL TIME

Ya Tsing and David Cheng watched each other carefully as they left the local gym for their weekly noon volleyball game. It was important not to change their routine in the least, but they needed to act as quickly as possible.

Neither had been able to sleep properly the night before, and even carrying on all day at work had been a challenge. So when they left the gym sweating and tired, they pretended not to show any signs of fatigue or worry. They made sure they always played on opposing sides, and joshed as they always had, patting each other on the back after their strenuous competition. It was time for a shower, and the two of them saw a chance to talk privately.

David was especially anxious as he had mentioned the B word "bioweapon" to Tchao Suk Dong two days ago, and although Director Tchao had *appeared* to think it was all a big joke, one could never be sure of Director Tchao. There was just something about him that David could not describe; it was rather something he *felt*. Tchao appeared to be very fond of him but was he? Was he being watched or was that paranoia on his part?

David stripped down quickly and wrapped himself in a towel as he hid behind a locker pretending to do something. He noted that Ya Tsing was doing the same thing, even motioning to one of his teammates to go along to the showers and he would not hesitate to come.

As soon as the last teammate hit the showers, David checked all over for cameras and ran over to Ya Tsing, whispering,

"Quick. We need to destroy all the work at the lab!"

"Duh. But the data's in ten separate sets of files. One set for each lab."

"Jesus."

"But the good thing about the data files is that there's no back-up, no second or third version either," said Ya Tsing.

"Why would they be so careless?" said David looking around again, at the ceilings, at the walls, even running out near the showers to make sure someone wasn't coming out.

"David, stay here, we're allowed to talk. If someone or a camera even saw you looking around like that, you'd look really suspicious. Calm down," said Ya Tsing. "It isn't carelessness. They did it on purpose so that only Tchao will ever know the full picture of what they are developing."

"That's funny," said David. "Tchao himself said he never mentioned what work one lab was doing to another lab, but for me he would make an exception."

"That's why we gotta work fast," said Ya Tsing. "I figure it'll take five minutes to identify and delete each file. That totals fifty minutes, but I estimate it will only take thirty minutes before the system realizes that security has been breached, and that the real Tchao Suk Dong is not accessing his files," added Ya Tsing.

"Right, but that's why we plan to go in at night when the lab is deserted."

"Sure David! You think that's easy? Not really. We will be able to access the main door at the rear of the building, but we won't be able to get through the steel gate. The steel gate cannot be opened at night."

David ran to the shower and then to the window to make sure no one was coming out, "I'll have to figure that one out. And then I will only have fifty minutes to destroy the files and only thirty minutes before the alarm goes off. Will I have enough time?" David was looking feverishly at him as if he were the Holy Grail.

"Maybe David, but there will be a security detail on its way to the lab."

"Will I have enough time before they arrive?"

"Maybe. If not, you're finished."

"Quick, let's get in the showers before people become suspicious."

David walked quietly over to enter the showers. Ya Tsing followed him, a distant second.

CHAPTER TWENTY-SEVEN – "HELP"

Bonnie was looking very good. Leaning on the countertop, she was sporting a tight-fitting, low-cut, green army tank top, a black Levi's belt specially fitted for small caliber bullets, a pair of taupe green fatigues and black army boots. Her body moved sensually as she shifted weight and listed the following items on her cell phone:

- Rope
- Lightweight, extendable thirty-foot ladder
- Night vision goggles
- Long distance microphone,
- Rifle and more ammo
- Two identical high-speed motor bikes (rentals)
- 4 crash helmets
- Pick-up truck rental

"That should do it," she said to herself.

"You are so hot!"

"Oh-h-h!" she jumped, as she looked up to see David who had been standing there for a while staring at her. She smiled slyly at him as he came up to give her more than a kiss and a feel.

"Not the time now, hon', business calls." She pronounced it /bidness/ to give her a tough tone because that's what she need to be now: tough. She returned David's very sensual kiss and neutralized his groping hands to say,

"Come on, hon', we got errands to run." She nodded for him to precede her.

As David reluctantly walked ahead, she grabbed an overlarge heavy leather coat and wrapped it around her shoulders. She wanted to hide the fact that she was not only a tour guide, but also a soldier. Then she quietly slid open a kitchen drawer and pulled out a large meat-carving knife and slid it into the breast pocket of her jacket. David paused and looked back. He didn't notice her knife.

"Coming?" he said.

"Of course," she smiled as she zipped up her coat and overtook him.

Thirty minutes later while they were exiting their bank and walking towards their car, they saw that the street was almost deserted. This was strange in itself because usually there were more people about. Bonnie looked quickly all around and noticed only one policeman on the opposite side of the street. His right hand was resting on his handgun, and he seemed to be returning Bonnie's stare.

A young man began walking quickly towards them on their side of the street. He held his right hand in his pocket and had his eyes completely fixated on David.

Bonnie unzipped her coat and let it hang open. She felt for her instrument to make sure it was still there. Then she grabbed David's arm, drew him in close and whispered,

"When I shout 'now,' run into the roadway."

"What?"

Bonnie kept her eyes concentrated on the man's right hand. She could see his knife as he came closer. When he was three feet away, he thrust the knife towards David's stomach.

"Now!"

In one movement, Bonnie pushed David and thrust her kitchen knife into the young man's right arm. The man yelped and ran away.

Bonnie grabbed David's arm and forced him to keep walking. She started walking faster and faster and David had to half-run to keep up. Finally, they came to a park and disappeared inside.

Bonnie looked back. The cop had disappeared. If he had been a normal cop, he would have pursued all players in this knifing; instead he disappeared.

"Bonnie, what just happened?"

"They were going to assassinate you. The kid with the knife was going to stick you and the cop had orders to take out the kid. Each got separate orders and were following them to a "T." It was all pre-planned to ensure the killing was not traced back to your employers."

"Come again?"

"David. They are on to us or at least *you*. We need to act. Now! And we need your volleyball bud Ya Tsing and his girlfriend."

CHAPTER TWENTY-EIGHT – SLEEPLESS IN WUHAN

Wuhan, China, 1 am

David Cheng was lying with his hands under his head on the right side of the bed staring out the picture window looking over the Yangtze. His special cushion—a "My Pillow" he had bought when he was last in the US—wasn't doing him any good now. Normally, he'd hit that medium-firm pillow and would be asleep in under three minutes. But that was an hour and a half ago. Since then he had been listening to the soft purring sound of Bonnie from her left side of the bed.

At least she wasn't a snorer. He could have found a girlfriend with a sinus condition. Thank God she was not one of them. Bonnie was the perfect woman: an alpha female in a beta package. *But why did she have to be CIA? He couldn't have it both ways, right?* David longed for a time when he would be ignorant of everything going on around him—ignorance was bliss. It seemed like an eternity since he had been working diligently on finding a vaccine; but it was only since

Bonnie had told him he was *an assignment,* or ridiculous words to that effect, that he had changed his attitude towards her. He needed to get over that and be less sensitive for he wouldn't have met her otherwise. He looked over at this cutie all curled up like a little bear on her own "My Pillow." She didn't look like the licensed killer in skintight army fatigues he had seen the other day. And now she was the only one sleeping.

Why couldn't David be as relaxed? For one thing, if he were to get caught during their break-in, he might spend ninety-nine years in prison. He would die there. And what would his parents go through? They would die of shame and remorse. Especially his father in whom he confided everything. *And therefore he couldn't involve his father in this; Papa would lose his job.*

***

Not too far away and at the same time, Xi Di Wan lay alone and wide awake in her sheer black panties; she was staring up at the ceiling mirror. She was in love with herself—or was it her body—but she was not happy. *Right now, an imposter, an intruder was lying next to David Cheng,* someone she should have taken out when she'd had the chance, before this American bitch had dug her hooks into him.

She ran her fingers over her panties, feeling the brillo pad hidden below perched atop her mons pubis. And then she ran them over her heavy breasts anchoring her nipples, erect as always, especially when she thought her nasty thoughts which was constantly, especially when she thought of David. And now he would have to go, *what a shame*, but she would have to do what she had to do. Even at this late hour, there was always time to call for a 6 am raid by the Chinese SWAT team. They would root out those two cockroaches, and she would lead the charge! She would have to get up at 5 am, at least, or *maybe not even go to bed at all*?

***

David was dreaming now—he kept telling himself he couldn't sleep—as he walked alone along the juniper-laden pathways at Stanford. It was hot, but dry, California hot, and the light was intense, shadowed only by the eucalyptus trees next to the Epidemiology Department,

"I see you working at the WHO one day, David," said Dr. Reinhardt.

"You really think so, Sir?" said David, as Jesse Owens, walked up and joined them.

"Maybe both of you will be working there?" said Dr. Reinhardt, "but right now it's volleyball time, right?"

"Hello, Dr. Reinhardt?" said Jesse, "what's this about?"

"David will tell you," said Dr. Reinhardt walking away, "Have a good game, guys." Reinhardt walked off and Jesse Owens said, "What was that all about?"

"Let's just say that Dr. Reinhardt thinks we really have bright futures, maybe at the WHO one day?"

"*Okay? O-kay?* You ready to play?"

"Sure, let's do it."

They ran off, and in David's mind a wave of nostalgia washed over him and slammed into the reality of the big picture window and the Yangtze river lying straight out there. David shuddered and yelped slightly.

Bonnie stirred and rolled over facing David, but then her regular breathing resumed. David had *almost dozed off there*, he told himself. But now he was wide awake again. It wasn't fair that Bonnie was allowed to sleep. Why couldn't he?

***

This American bitch is a cougar, totally different from me!, laughed Xi. *What a name she goes by, "Bonnie," how ridiculous! Her real name is Isabelle Renault, like the car, a cheap brand. If I torture her, which is what I will do, she'll become a martyr, and attract sympathy. One thing the CIA does not need is sympathy. But I can't underestimate her. She's smart, the way she outwitted that cop and his decoy yesterday. Then she got David to a safehouse, and I'll have to figure out where that is. As soon as I see her, I'll blow her head off, no need to mess about.*

***

Bonnie moved again, her purring stopped, then started again as her regular breathing resumed. *Can she be trusted? She has been lying to me for the past eight months.* There was something about her, though, hibernating like a bear under the covers, camped out on her side of the bed. Bonnie didn't just hang out or flop about on the bed: either, she slept by herself or she fucked like a minks; there was no in-between. *The fact was that tomorrow's, make that today's, operation totally depended on her.* He would have to totally trust her. Of that he could be sure!

***

Xi Di Wan ran her fingers lightly over her Mound of Venus again. She could feel that stirring from the beast within, that stirring that overcame her brain and made her make rash choices. It was her Achilles heel; it wasn't just men that thought with their dicks. She realized she wouldn't involve the police because there could be no publicity about what they were developing at the lab. She was her father's right-hand woman, and he was the head of the operation so he could be trusted, but could she trust the two lab security men that worked under her? Her father provided them to her, but now she had to control them! She liked to control men, she had to admit, and when there wasn't one in her bed, she was able to contain her moods, but it wasn't easy. She grabbed "Big Mac" from her night table and imagined it was David as she vibrated herself to the top of Mount Venus, and then slept the sleep of the wicked.

***

Bonnie awoke with a start and in a sweat. She had been moaning for some time and suddenly cried out in anguish, "David, we were running and running and—

"And?" said David, immediately wrapping her in his arms, "And?"

"And what? What are you doing awake?" she suddenly realized.

"I couldn't sleep."

Bonnie pulled away from him to look at the clock on her night table. It was 2 am, "You haven't been able to sleep for two and a half hours!" she said as she snuggled up to him again.

"Well, maybe I dozed off there for a bit," he smiled, "but mostly no, I couldn't sleep."

"I think I know why," she smiled, and with that she slid down his body and went to work.

■■■

CHAPTER TWENTY-NINE - SABOTAGE

In the early morning light, Xi Di Wan stood in front of her full-length mirror and admired her "blackness." From her panties and brassiere to her tight-fitting black cotton tank top, she was the Cat Woman in waiting, ready for action. She zipped up her black leather jacket and shook her shiny, shoulder-length black hair. Her look needed a touch of color so she applied a little rouge to her lips to go with the discreet, blood-red ribbon in her hair.

Her phone beeped to signal that her two henchmen had just pulled up in their dark blue Mercedes G class jeep and were waiting for her. She shouldered her black *Eastpak* backpack, containing rope, knives, bullets, pliers and handcuffs, and all easily organized for immediate use. She strapped on a thick black belt packed with ammo and two Luger pistols,

"Let's get 'em, Bonnie!" she said out loud in English.

***

"It's time, David," said Bonnie, shaking her lover awake at 5 am. He had slept soundly for four hours after Bonnie had intervened and now jumped up, full of energy and ready for all the action a twenty-three-year-old could summon. After a quick wash and something to eat, David got dressed and packed his gear. They looked round the room to make sure they hadn't forgotten anything when Bonnie said,

"How do they know where we are all the time?"

"Who?"

"You know, the bad guys? Like the other day when they tried to kill you? How do they know?" David thought a moment,

"I'm sure I would have seen if the lab had put a tracker on me."

"You sure, David? Did they give you something with a tracker in it?" David shook his head and then picked up his Huawei smartphone and put it in his pocket,

"That phone, David? Where did you buy it?"

"I didn't. Oh no, it was a gift from Tchao Suk Dong!"

"Leave it here. Just take your other cell phone."

They crept outside making as little noise as possible and staying away from the lit-up areas where possible in the hazy morning. Using high-powered flashlights, they quickly checked over their rental pick-up truck, outside and in, to see if it had been tampered with. They carefully searched the pre-loaded extension ladder. Then, they left the apartment and drove it the short distance to the lab.

Bonnie stopped the pick-up truck on the street outside the lab. Both she and David jumped out, grabbed their gear and climbed onto its flat bed. Bonnie whipped on her headphones, switched on her laptop and scanned the still black sky with an omni-directional microphone,

"Got the readings!" She checked them and said,

"Position your flashlight there and scan the sky." David did so and she whispered,

"A bit to the left and then go back to the same position, ok?" She grabbed a silencer-equipped, long-range rifle and aimed,

"Now!" David moved his flashlight back to illuminate a drone watching the lab building and Bonnie fired one shot. *Swoosh!*

"Bulls-eye!" she hissed.

"I didn't know you were an American sniper," he said.

"A lot of things you don't know, nerdy, but I still love you!" They lifted the ladder and climbed down from the truck. Bonnie stopped,

"What's the matter, Bonnie?"

"Shhh, can you hear it? Quick! Back on the truck. There's another drone. We gotta find it and take it out!"

They dropped their ladder on the ground, jumped back on the truck, and Bonnie donned her headphones and hit a few keys on her laptop. The position of a second drone appeared and David knew what to do. He waited for her to aim her rifle, and then shone his flashlight where the drone was, illuminating it. Bonnie took her shot; again, only one shot was needed,

"Bingo!" The drone went down.

David positioned the articulating rubber feet of the twenty-five-foot extension ladder at the front of the building. When he adjusted the feet so the ladder couldn't slip, he pulled on the sash cords to hoist up the smaller part and extend it to the top of the building.

Without thinking, David climbed up the rungs quickly with two long ropes over his shoulder and grappling hooks. At twenty feet up, David's fear of heights made him freeze,

"I can't do this, Bonnie!"

"Of course you can, you have to. Don't look down and don't think about the height. Just about the next step."

"Easy for you to say. I can't stop thinking I'm about to fall!"

"Shut the hell up, David! Just do it!"

He eventually got up to the roof and secured one of the grappling hooks to the front of the building and threw the rope down. He walked across the roof to the rear and anchored the other grappling hook. Then, he threw that rope down to enable him to climb down to the ground.

But then his vertigo kicked in and he was afraid of getting on the rope to go down. Bonnie was worried he was taking so long and got him on the phone,

"Come on, hon', concentrate on the job at hand. Look only at the rope, make sure that is tight, hold on to the roof with one hand and the rope with the other. Don't look down!"

David pocketed his phone and did as he was told with a great deal of trepidation. As soon as he climbed down, she removed the extension ladder and put it on the truck. She wanted to make sure a passing drone would be less likely to see anything unusual at the building.

"Hurry up, David, a replacement drone will be here any second."

Bonnie stayed with the truck and David entered the main entrance and, after an iris scan, entered the lab.

***

Around the same time and equipped with battering rams and tools, Xi Di Wan and her two henchmen passed through the five security entrances to David and Bonnie's apartment using Xi's access card. Inside the elevator, Cat Woman said,

"You two grab David and cuff him to the bed. I'll take care of the bitch!"

In front of the apartment, Xi pulled out her twenty-eight-ounce construction hammer and lopped off the doorknob. Xi's associates rammed the remaining lock and forced open the door. Cat Woman ran in,

"Where the fuck are they!" she screamed in Mandarin. Then she saw David's Huawei and collapsed to her knees.

***

Back in the lab, David rushed to his computer and looked around. No one else was there so early; he was lucky. He checked his watch and set the timer for fifty minutes. He had ten files to delete permanently. He booted up his computer and ran through the protocols. He found the first file and deleted it. A few minutes later, he found the second. He deleted that as well. It wasn't always going to be this easy, but he started breathing more calmly. Three and four were much more difficult but eventually, he was able to delete those as well. Number five was a bitch but he finally got through that.

He was blowing hard and sweating just as much; big saddlebag perspiration stains hung down from his armpits. Thirty minutes struck and David noticed a big "ALARM" written on the screen. He had deleted seven files, three more to go. Theoretically, he had twenty minutes left but now that there was an "ALARM" signal, security would be there in no more than ten minutes.

***

One of Xi Di Wan's henchmen shouted,

"There's been a break-in at the lab!" Xi who had been tearing down pictures of David and Bonnie together, regrouped and yelled,

"Quick, let's go!"

They barreled out of the apartment, through the five gates and out into their Mercedes G class jeep.

***

Back at the lab, David was frantically hitting different keys and clicking madly. Bonnie wouldn't stop chattering through the earbuds connected to his phone,

"Shut the fuck up, Bonnie! I can't concentrate!"

"Sorry, hon'" and she went silent.

The big red letters "ACCESS DENIED" kept appearing on his black screen. But David wouldn't quit, he was on a roll. He kept hitting keys and "Return," more keys and "Return." Then other keys, the same thing, no access. Finally, he hit "Return" and his screen went green. "ACCESS GRANTED" in big white letters on an emerald-green screen. He deleted the last file,

"Done," he said to Bonnie.

Then he noticed that next to six pressurized oxygen cylinders was a canister of extremely flammable liquid. He ran to the kitchen frantically searching for matches.

"Get out!" ran through his earbuds as Bonnie started jumping up and down on her end and David, who had found some matches, missed his first strike because he was shaking so much. This was fortunate for him because he had to run back to his computer to find the control system for the sprinkler system and disable it,

"Get out!" Bonnie screamed again through his earbuds.

David ran back to the oxygen cylinders and threw a match into the container of flammable liquid and ran as he'd never run before back to the rope. High on adrenaline, he climbed the rope with no fear, ran across the roof to the front wall, checked the grappling hooks and grabbed the other rope. This time, he forgot about his vertigo and expertly scaled down to halfway when he was overcome with panic about being too slow. Holding on with both hands, he let the rope burn his hands as he tried to stop his downward motion. He jammed his legs as he hit the ground too hard but Bonnie helped him up and they ran to the truck.

There was an explosion in the building and they were thrown to the ground.

They managed to stand up and scramble into the pick-up and drive off just as Xi's Mercedes G class jeep approached and passed them by.

CHAPTER THIRTY – NO WUHAN, NO FLY

A short time later.

It was still dark so David and Bonnie coasted in their pick-up for the last five hundred yards with their lights off so as not to attract attention; they turned into a hotel parking lot. They limped into their pre-paid room and shut the door. They held on to each other, shaking, and laughing. They had done it, and were safe, but for how long?

They tore off their clothes, showered and checked each other out for cuts, bruises and dried blood. David's feet were bruised and he had rope burns on his hands, as well as multiple cuts from flying glass shards. Bonnie not only had creams and disinfectant, she also had make-up for both of them so as not to attract suspicion when they would leave their room a few hours later. Neither had slept well, but after their adrenaline high, they were exhausted so they set their alarm and collapsed on the bed.

11 am came soon enough with each of them jumping out of opposite sides of the bed to the shrill

alarm. It was time to get going; they could only hide for so long. Bonnie had not only pre-paid for this short term "safe house," she had seen to all the details. She had packed two large backpacks containing spare clothes, phone chargers, their passports and airline tickets, as well as two leather "biker" suits, one for her and one for David! She had also rented a Suzuki motorcycle which was waiting in the parking lot. Bonnie had seen to that as well.

When they were all cleaned up, they donned their black leather biker suits and backpacks, and ran out to their motorcycle. David got on first.

"I was going to drive. Do you know how, David?"

"Of course. When I was at Stanford, we used to take bikes up to the mountains and terrify rattlesnakes." He looked over at their parked pick-up,

"We'd better remove those plates so they can't trace us quickly."

"I'm on it!" Bonnie whipped out a rivet gun from her backpack and removed the plates before David had even finished getting used to the settings on the bike.

They discarded the truck license plates and their old clothes in a nearby dumpster. They were about to mount their motorcycle when Bonnie stopped cold.

"Wait!" said Bonnie, "We need to go back to the apartment."

"Now? They'll be waiting for us?"

"Maybe not. We need your Huawei to make sure the diversion goes well."

David and Bonnie, dressed in identical leather motorcycle suits, went through the five security gates and ran up the stairs up rather than take the elevator. They cautiously approached their front door which had been rammed open in the early morning. The Huawei was still in the same spot, so they grabbed it and ran back to the bike!

***

Xi Di Wan was in her apartment. She was still asleep in her black leather get-up from the morning. Her laptop had been left on all night with a video connection to her two security men dozing away in their Mercedes G class Jeep outside on the street.

Suddenly, the men jumped up in their seats as their video feed started beeping. Almost instantaneously, Xi jumped up as her driver yelled out,

"They're on the move again!"

"Well, go out and get 'em!" Xi replied automatically as she arose from her stupor and ran to the bathroom.

A little round icon with "Huawei" written on it was moving away from David and Bonnie's apartment on her phone map. On her other computer, Xi programmed another drone to follow the dynamic couple on the Suzuki.

Within a minute, a split screen from both drones revealed two figures in black leather on a Suzuki motorcycle speeding through Huanzi Lake along the road to Linjiao Lake. Xi reasoned they were driving north of Wuhan to the airport to leave the country, especially in the light of what had happened that morning and the direction they were taking. She started barking orders through her phone to Xi's driver who screeched out of there, burning a lot of rubber in the process,

"Cut them off at Tangjiaduncun!" she screamed through the car's loudspeaker. Xi's driver and his colleague laughed at their hysterical boss and accelerated dangerously through the Jianghan District, narrowly missing a local merchant on a bicycle on her way to the outdoor market. Through her monitor, Xi Di Wan thought she saw a motorcycle overtake a truck on a flyover crossing the big freeway and started gesticulating at her screen,

"Follow that motorcycle!" she screamed through the car loudspeaker. "I think they're going to the Wuhan Airport Toll Gate in the Huangpi District because they're not too far from Gusaoshucun."

***

Meanwhile, David and Bonnie realized that a Merc Jeep was gaining on them so they pulled into

Jinyintan and started taking side streets on their motorcycle that were much too narrow for the oversized G class Jeep. They would eventually lose the Merc except for one thing: Bonnie noticed they were also being tracked by two drones. She hadn't expected anything less. Retrieving that phone had perhaps been more trouble than it was worth but hopefully the risk was going to pay off.

Bonnie and David went down a narrow street and temporarily lost the security men who had to go around the block to find them. The dynamic duo skirted out of the dense city streets and pulled over out of sight of the security men at a flyover at Duyi Han. Ya Tsing and his girlfriend had just arrived on an identical motorcycle. They were both dressed in the same black leather as Bonnie and David. Bonnie had planned this whole ruse! Out of sight of the drones and under cover of the flyover, David handed off his Huawei to Ya Tsing. The Huawei would become David and Bonnie's decoy.

As planned by Bonnie, Ya Tsing and his girlfriend rode off in the opposite direction to the airport, and the security men, egged on by a hysterical Xi Di Wan through their loudspeaker, gave chase. So did one of the drones tracking the Huawei. The second drone did not follow the first because Xi had overridden its settings with her computer and was controlling it manually.

Suddenly Xi's father appeared on her screen. He was looking awful,

"I went to the lab this morning, Di Wan. What a disaster! Everything was destroyed. I don't know what happened!"

"I heard. It was David Cheng. I know it was."

"David! Surely not! I thought you were going to take him out?"

"We almost did, but—"

"Di Wan, it's over. There is no more Wuhan Project!"

"I'm going to get those bastards, David and his girlfriend, if it's the last thing I do!"

"Please, Di Wan, forget it. We need to cover our asses now. I'll work out a story for the press."

"No, Father. What he did was the last straw. It's personal now. As they say in America, it's never over till it's over, and till the fat lady sings."

Now all this time, Bonnie and David had remained under the flyover, invisible to the drone and thus to Xi Di Wan and her henchmen. Meanwhile, Ya Tsing and his girlfriend were leading Xi's security men on a joy ride; into greater Wuhan and out again, sometimes going in the direction of the airport and then away again in a different direction. They were very aware of the Mercedes G class Jeep following them and made sure to always remain in front of them but to "tease" them. *Who was chasing whom!* Finally, they rode towards the river and parked the motorcycle behind a tree near a park. They jumped out before the Jeep could catch up with them. Then, they spread a picnic blanket on the grassy riverbank and sat down to watch the road.

A half hour went by and Ya Tsing looked at his watch,

"That should be enough time for those two."

After a moment, they saw the two men that had been following them in the Mercedes G class come towards them and then stop suddenly. One of them pulled out his cellphone while they stood there, staring at Ya Tsing and girlfriend from about fifty yards,

"Xi, we don't understand," said the driver. "We found them, but they're not the same people, they're not Bonnie and David."

"How can that be?" said Xi through the earbuds.

Xi saw movement on her computer screen from the other drone,

"Hold on!" She followed the movement and a picture of a new motorcycle and two people dressed in black appeared. They were heading for the airport.

"*What!* I don't understand!...Oh no, oh no-o-o-o! Shit! Shit!" She hung up and started looking around for her Lugers,

"Oh, fuck, I left them in the Mercedes!"

"Xi Di Wan, Xi Di Wan??" The driver clicked his cellphone to call back but Xi didn't respond. Fifteen seconds later, she yelled,

"Forget those people! They're of no interest! We've been tricked."

She overrode the automatic settings for her "drone spies" and set the two of them to manual, only to realize that Bonnie and David were approaching the Airport Road toll gate and were about to go into the airport. She grabbed her bag of martial arts weapons and mumbled to herself,

"Never send in a boy to do a woman's job!"

CHAPTER THIRTY-ONE – CLAWS!

Bonnie and David sped past Majia Lake and into Zongfengjia Ju at the entrance of the Wuhan Tianhe International Airport. David was about to park their motorcycle in short term parking when Bonnie called through her microphone to David's headset in his helmet,

"I don't think so. Keep going to the back end of this airport where there's a heart-shaped road surrounding the Terminal 1 and 2 parking lots. We can't risk the main entrance in case they are watching."

"What do you mean?" David answered back through his microphone, all the while accelerating back out of the main entrance and heading for the ring road, "Ya Tsing and his girlfriend are our decoys. There's no way they know we're here."

"I wouldn't be too sure," said Bonnie through clenched teeth, "Xi Di Wan is no dope, and she's probably figured out where we are." David drove around the airport.

"Okay, we're at the back entrance now," said David.

Bonnie got her bearings and said,

"Inch over by that storm drain, and we'll leave the bike here. Over there is the blocked off back entrance. We'll go there."

"Exactly," said David as if he were the evil scientist in the "Gold Member" James Bond spoofs, "why go in the easy front way with no hassle when you can navigate thirty-foot-wide storm drains twenty-five feet deep and break in the back way?"

"Come on, you wuss, it's easy. There's a bridge across that storm drain! Look, over there!"

"Sure, Bonnie, it's three feet wide and no handrail. And that's no storm drain. It's like a swimming pool it's so big. Take your helmet off!"

By this time, David had parked the bike and removed his helmet while Bonnie was still looking around appraising the terrain. This was no storm drain; it looked more like a huge moon crater, and there was a narrow steel-reinforced wooden bridge running down the side of it with no ropes or handrails and a twenty-five-foot drop to the concrete bottom. She figured most of the operatives worked the bottom of the drain repairing it but some needed to reach the top to go into the airport, and hence the small bridge over this "swimming pool." *But why make it so big so you couldn't get through to the back entrance? And where are the workers? No one was around!* She looked at her watch and realized it was their lunch hour. *That's lucky for us!* Bonnie pulled her helmet off and looked at David and laughed,

"Come on, Spider Man, I saw you jumping over roofs this morning. You can manage a thirty-foot-long bridge!"

David inched his way onto the steel-reinforced wooden bridge, froze, and then inched his way back.

"No way!" he told Bonnie.

David checked his phone for any news on the lab as if something, *anything*, would serve as an excuse to not cross the bridge! He pulled a News App up on his smartphone and clicked on the "speaker" icon so he and Bonnie could hear the breaking news in Chinese:

"The Wuhan Research Institute of China suffered a devastating explosion early this morning. Fortunately, there were no deaths and no one was injured as it happened during the night and no one was there. Authorities believe that the explosion was due to a gas leak. Director Tchao Suk Dong was not available to comment as he had just left for Switzerland en route to resolve an urgent matter in Nigeria, Africa. However, he did leave a general message for the media saying how unfortunate it had been for all the dedicated researchers who had spent years fighting viruses and were now out of work. He himself expected to be in Africa for at least a year."

"Very convenient for him, taking a year's sabbatical. Especially today, isn't it?" said Bonnie, laughing.

Suddenly the constant rumble of passing traffic on the ring road was interrupted when a motorcycle jumped the barrier and landed on dry earth. It slammed on its brakes and the tires screeched as it came to a stop about twenty yards away. A cloud of dust formed and from it strode a leather-clad figure brandishing her martial arts weapons.

David didn't notice this figure and asked rhetorically,

"I guess we're in the clear? Can't we go through the main entrance now?"

"No David, you can't. You're a back-door man, remember? Run away, little man, while I kill your bitch."

It was Xi Di Wan who had just pulled up in her own Harley.

She took a run at Bonnie but missed with a front snap kick to her solar plexus when Bonnie faked right and then went left. Bonnie quickly pulled out a knife to cut her throat, but Xi was too quick and kicked it out of her hand. David then charged her, but Xi kicked him hard in the nuts, almost crippling him.

"Get across that bridge, David. Now!" Bonnie shouted.

"Yes, David, run along, and let us women claw it out!"

There was nothing else David could do in the condition he was in, so he literally crawled onto the rickety, steel-reinforced wooden bridge, looking straight ahead to the back entrance so as not to fall into the storm drain.

The warrior ladies were now exchanging front snap and roundhouse kicks as Xi tried to maneuver Bonnie towards the edge of the crater. But Bonnie was no slouch at martial arts either and managed to land an "empi" elbow to Xi's solar plexus that missed but stung her in her left boob. Xi winced and tried to claw Bonnie's eyes out with a Kung Fu maneuver but missed again as Bonnie ducked and bloodied Xi's forehead with a head butt. And on they went, with Xi's superior technique a slight advantage over Bonnie's tremendous athletic ability and balance.

Xi maneuvered Bonnie to the edge of the crater so the only choice Bonnie had was to take to the bridge after David, who was still crawling along because of his bruised balls. Xi rushed onto the bridge forgetting there was no handrail and thinking she could push Bonnie off, but the taller American jumped up and aimed a high snap "crane" kick to Xi's chin à la Karate Kid. Xi's head snapped back; she lost her balance and fell off the bridge, only to catch hold of one of the planks and hold on at the last second. She dangled there with one hand, her four fingers showing off her black nail polish and her thumb badly bloodied waiting for Bonnie to finish her off.

Bonnie ran back to do just that but hesitated, and then walked away to rejoin David who had finally reached the back entrance,

"You cunt! Just you wait. I'll get you. I won't show you any mercy! Nice guys finish last. You Americans are weak. We Chinese are far superior and we will beat you! You'll see."

"Can you believe this bitch!" Bonnie said to David, "Who's the one hanging by a thread?"

"Why didn't you finish her off?"

"Come on, David, we've saved millions of lives. What's one more?" Bonnie said grabbing her lover by the hand, "we've got a plane to catch!"

EPILOGUE

September 2019

That morning it was warm and hazy, but Hee So Sik did what he always did at 6:30 am: he jumped on his bicycle and rode from the poor part of town where he lived with his wife and three young children, crossed the Yangtze and coasted into the Wuhan Industrial Park. Once there, he would pass the car seat and tire factories, the pen factory, and finally a huge toy firm before he turned into the Wuhan Research Institute of China.

But where was the WRIC! It was no more! What was going on?

Hee So Sik looked around, checked the street signs to make sure he was in the right area and gazed up at the destruction. He wiped away some snot from his nose and coughed a few times. He still wasn't well; was he seeing things?

A whole façade of the building was black from a fire or explosion of some sort. That must have happened yesterday when he had to miss work because he wasn't feeling well, and even today, he wasn't in great shape.

Nobody had told him about this explosion, and now hordes of police were putting yellow tape around the area and huge bulldozers stood at the ready behind large "Demolition" signs.

What was he going to do? He wasn't feeling well and didn't want to get involved with the police so he decided to call one of his friends from home. He trusted them more.

Hee So Sik was about to leave when he saw another sign, "Coming soon. A new facility for China Sunshine Soap Company. *We are hiring.*" What! They were opening a soap company at the site of the lab? He was a cleaner and they were hiring? So this was some good news! Maybe he would get this new job? Or maybe he would get his old job back if they rebuilt the facility, *and hopefully at a higher salary*? All the same, it was too bad about the research lab. He noted the web address for CSSC, and decided to send them a letter for a job once he got home.

He blinked a few times. His eyes were watering, so maybe it was a good thing he didn't have to work today. Especially his right eye that was really very sore.

Why didn't Director Tchao Suk Dong call me and everyone else in the company?

He pedaled away, but then remembered he needed to get some food at the Wuhan Wet Market. He had seen some good fresh minks, fox, dog and bat there the other day, but no fish. His good friend, Tchi Tchou Yu, who served at the meat counter, would give him a good deal. Maybe there would even be fish today.

"Hey Tchou Yu, how goes the world?" Hee So Sik said. He coughed hard and wiped his nose on his hands and then on his pants.

"Better for me than for you, it seems!" Tchi Tchou Yu said. "You look like you should be in bed! You're sweating like one of my pigs back there, even though it's very mild today. We don't have much fish today. But we have a good selection of bats: Indian flying fox, Honduran whites, and a few Egyptian fruit bats. What would you like?"

"I actually wanted fish but I'll take some of that raccoon meat and a little minks."

"I got some good bat soup if you want?" Tchi Tchou Yu said, "It's delicious!"

"Nahh, never liked bat soup. Anyway, bats are dangerous. Carry a lot of disease."

"You should talk, Hee So Sik! We disinfect them first. You work in a research lab!"

"You mean, I clean a research lab. I am totally protected. I'm completely covered head to toe, mask, surgical gloves, face shield, special boots. I wear three different suits that I keep for each lab, and then I have my street clothes."

After this loud pronouncement about how careful he was, Hee So Sik had a fleeting thought he might not be telling the full truth. His right eye was getting worse and worse. He started coughing into his hand and wiped the gook onto his pants so that his hands were dry. Then he peeled off a few bills from his thick wad of cash and paid for the raccoon and minks meat.

"And look at you! You're as sick as a dog, and you're touching that money! I hope it's not infected" said the merchant.

"Hey, Tchi Tchou Yu," answered Hee So Sik, "everybody touches money! Money is one of the dirtiest things I know!"

"Aside from people's mouths!" answered Tchi Tchou Yu, "Money is the root of all evil. Give me a bite of the root!"

And they laughed their partially toothless laughs, and Hee So Sik coughed his dry cough as he shook Tchi Tchou Yu's hand and walked away.

One month later, they were both dead.

THE END

Printed in Great Britain
by Amazon

45738088R00130